ADVANCE PRAISE FOR REFUGE ON THE MOUNTAIN

For fans of post-apocalyptic survival stories, Refuge On the Mountain is an absolute belter of a novel. Cornelia Feye spins a gripping yarn full of suspense, action, and thrills, where each chapter brings new nail-biting moments that will have you on the edge of your seat. Capitalizing on an intriguing premise, Feye takes readers through a narrative filled to the brim with tension and drama to keep you hooked until the end. The plot moves at a brisk pace, twisting and turning in ways you never see coming. Each character has a distinct personality, and the inter-relationship dynamics add to the enjoyment of the story with layers to peel back. As a reader who loves post-apocalyptic survival stories, this one was right up my alley, and I can't recommend it highly enough.

~Pikasho Deka, Readers' Favorite 5-star review

Set in the near future, Cornelia Feye has created a gripping post-apocalyptic mystery story that pits good against evil and is true to human nature. As in her prior work, Feye's characters, from a variety of backgrounds are well-drawn, believable, and complex. This exciting work begins as an CME (Coronal Mass Ejection) throws the world as we know it into a struggle to survive. When the body of a murdered man is found on the trail, Greg Stern, in an effort to protect his family, makes the decision to hide the body and not report the murder. Feye masterfully reveals the cast of characters and their foibles she takes the reader on an emotional ride of highs, lows, failures and successes. And, brings REFUGE ON THE MOUNTAIN, to a shocking conclusion. A must read for anyone who is intrigued by the idea that this talented writer can combine mystery, sci-fi, Zen Buddhism, and art history into a compelling read.

~Tamara Merrill, author of *Shadows in Our Bones*

Cornelia Feye crafts a compelling narrative that keeps the reader on the edge of their seat throughout the story. Cornelia expertly builds tension and suspense, creating a palpable sense of urgency as the characters face an unprecedented threat to their way of life. The interplay of family dynamics and the evolving relationships between the characters add depth to the plot, making it more than just a typical post-apocalyptic thriller. The characters are well-developed and relatable, making it easy to connect with their struggles and triumphs. From Greg and Vega's determination to protect their family to the complex dynamics within the group of survivors, the characters feel authentic and multi-dimensional. I enjoyed reading Refuge on the Mountain. This is a compelling and thought-provoking novel that seamlessly blends elements of post-apocalyptic fiction and murder mystery.

~Natalie Soine for Readers' Favorite, 5-star review

Refuge on the Mountain by Cornelia Feye is a post-apocalyptic narrative that features a compelling set of characters. I liked the diversity of the family whose members had different origins, yet were closely knit. Greg and Stevie were easy for me to identify with and provided a conventional point of view. Vega had a strong faith in her goddess which provided an alternate approach to life. Lin, Tarek, and Hilde were impressive survivors of racial prejudice and political unrest. I liked the way some invited people were considered non-family but proved essential to the plot. I enjoyed the twists and turns of the plot which brought assistance from unexpected sources and placed blame where I least anticipated. The story made me question my assumptions regarding race and equality. Overall, Refuge on the Mountain by Cornelia Feye is a thought-provoking speculative read.

~Cecelia Hopkins for Readers' Favorite, 5-star review

REFUGE ON THE MOUNTAIN

REFUGE ON THE MOUNTAIN

A POST-APOCALYPTIC MYSTERY

CORNELIA FEYE

KONSTELLATION
PRESS

Konstellation Press, San Diego

www.konstellationpress.com

Cover design: Scarlet Willette

Copyediting; Martin Roy Hill

ISBN: 979-8-9868432-7-8

To survivors: humans, animals, trees, coral reefs, eco-systems

1

DAY 0, MINUS 10 HOURS: GREG

"In ten hours, the world as we know it, is going to end," says an urgent voice in Greg's cell phone. He moves out of the sun's glare streaming into his office, to see the caller ID. Rakesh Patel, Greg's Silicon Valley computer-nerd friend, who now works in cyber security at the National Security Agency. He met Rakesh at a Zen retreat and remembers his odd kind of humor, but this is not funny.

"Greg, are you there?"

Apparently, Greg has taken too long recalling Rakesh and his resume.

"Rakesh, what are you talking about? Is this some kind of joke?"

"I shouldn't even be telling you this, and I don't have time to explain, but you better get your family out of town and bring as much food and gas as you can. Turn off all your electric systems, and hopefully I'll see you on the other side."

"Wait, what's going on?"

"A G5 level CME, the biggest since the Carrington Event. Look, I gotta go."

"How do you know about this?"

"NOAA warning satellites. It's confidential. Trust me and leave." He hangs up.

Greg stands dumbfounded looking at his black cell phone screen. What's a CME? A Google search informs him that a 'CME is a coronal mass ejection, or a significant release of plasma and accompanying magnetic field from the sun's corona into the heliosphere. When reaching the earth's magnetosphere, it can cause geomagnetic storms and damage to the power grid.' If it is large enough, it can fry the entire electric grid. For a very long time.

"Shit." If Rakesh is right, this is a global disaster. Rakesh is super smart, an expert in analyzing and identifying cyber-attacks. He's a big shot now, working for the government to identify threats to America's digital infrastructure. His information is probably accurate.

Greg sits down at his large wooden desk. It's cluttered with piles of papers and requests he should be dealing with to run his private security company. An image of a giant solar flare licking through space flashes through his mind. The flare reaches earth and burns the continent of

Australia. Greg shakes himself out of this nightmare vision. It is time to act.

"Vega," he calls his wife as he prepares to storm out of the office. "Pack up all the food we have and all the clothes you need for the next few months. We have to go up to the cabin immediately."

"What do you mean? I can't just drop everything. I have client meetings, I'm in the middle of ..."

"Stop Vega. There's no time. We have to get out. I'll call my mother and sister in Palm Springs. You call the boys and tell them to come to the cabin right away and bring food and clothing."

"Why? You make no sense."

"I'm coming home. We are on the brink of a global disaster. Tell the boys a CME is going to hit in ten hours. They'll understand."

"What does it mean? You're scaring me." Her voice is spiraling higher and higher. Greg doesn't want her to panic. Not now.

"Please Vega try to calm down, I'll explain later. We can't waste any time. I'll get supplies on my way."

"How do you know about this?"

"Rakesh told me. But it's strictly confidential."

Before she can say anything else, Greg hangs up the phone and walks out into the front office where his associate is working.

"Lisa, I have to leave for an emergency. You can take the day off."

"Why Mr. Stern?" She looks at him with astonishment and alarm.

"Just go home to your family."

"Are you sure?"

"Quite sure.

Minus 9 hours: **Vega**

With shaking hands, Vega dials Daniel's cell phone number. He's at the office of the Environmental Defense Council, where he is in charge of all technical and digital matters. He answers.

"What's up, mom? I'm at work."

"I know. Sorry to interrupt, but your dad says you have to come to the cabin right away and bring clothes and food."

"Why?"

"A CME or something is going to hit earth in nine hours."

"A CME? Did he say what level? G4 or G5?"

"You know what that is? Dad didn't have time to explain."

"It's a powerful solar storm, Mom. At the highest level the geomagnetic gamma rays destroy the entire global electric grid."

"I'm so confused. Is this a real thing? Can this really be happening? He says pack up clothes and all your food and shut everything off."

"It's real and plausible. Nine hours. Got it. I'm bringing Lin. I can't leave her behind. How does dad know?"

"Rakesh told him and it's confidential."

"Because of mass hysteria?"

"I don't know. What about all the people?"

"Start packing, mom. I'll see you at the ranch."

Daniel hangs up. Vega notices her pulse has accelerated to a fluttering pace. She runs her hands through her blonde hair. Daniel has confirmed the gravity of this event. A terrible, a global disaster. She takes a deep breath and calls her younger son, Stevie

MINUS 8 HOURS: **Downtown Los Angeles; Stevie**

"Guys, we're three shots behind schedule! Let's pulls this thing together! What's the matter with lighting? Adjust the spotlight on the dancers. What happened to Lee's make-up? Make-up people, fix the smudges under her eyes."

He looks around the spacious University of Southern California sound stage he rented for this music video. The band is getting restless, while the dancers put the finishing touches on their outfits and make-up. The drummer is doing a drum-roll to speed things up. The lead dancer in a skin-tight black leotard is doing cartwheels and a split to warm up for his routine. The three back-up singers in silver lamé costumes are giggling and fussing with their teased Donna Summer-style hairdos.

It's chaotic, but Stevie loves it. So much energy, so much talent, so much dynamic interaction, going in all different directions. It's his job to channel it all into a seamless performance and capture it in film. No mean feat, but when it happens, it's magic.

"Okay, we're ready ..."

His phone rings.

"Hold on—give me a second please!" Stevie picks up. "Mom, I can't talk. I'm in the middle of a production. It's crazy here."

His mom has no idea what it's like here, but he usually tries to answer her calls.

"Stevie, I know you're very busy, but your dad is adamant that you come up to the cabin immediately."

"That's impossible, we are already behind schedule!"

"This is an emergency."

"Did something happen?"

"A giant solar storm will hit earth."

Stevie looks around the set impatiently. The make-up person is fixing the smudge under Lee's eye.

"Stevie, catch the next train to San Diego asap. We'll meet you at the station."

"Mom, I'm producing a music video. I can't leave!" What is she thinking?

"A CME will strike in eight hours! If you don't come down here right away, we can't help you."

"What about my work? A lot of people depend on me here."

"Apparently no one will be able to watch your video once all the power is out!"

"Are you serious? How does he know?"

"It's a warning from NOAA, he knows it from a trustworthy source in the government."

"Shit, Mom, if that's true it is a catastrophe of global proportions!"

"Keep your voice down. We can't tell anybody!"

"Why? What will happen to all the people?"

"Stevie, we can't discuss this now, the time is ticking! Get here now."

"Okay, forget the train, I'm taking an Uber. I'll be there in a couple of hours."

Stevie disconnects his phone and looks around the soundstage. Actors, musicians, assistants, cameramen, sound and lighting crew, and hair/make up crew have fallen silent. They all look at him. He nervously touches the silver hoop in his ear and rubs the messy topknot of blond hair on his head. This is one of his first jobs since graduating from USC film school. He can't mess this up. But if his dad is right—and he's usually right …

"People, we're done for today. Go home to your families."

"What do you mean? We're right in the middle of this shoot," the lead dancer protests.

"I need to go. It's an emergency. You can continue without me, but I would go home to your families, if I was you."

Chaos erupts, voices rise in anger, people are shouting, protesting.

"Why? What's going on?"

Stevie doesn't have it in him to ignore them. "If this was your last day on earth, what would you do? Think about that and do it."

As if in a bubble of calm, he grabs his backpack with his computer and walks out onto the city street. He takes a good look around. The wind ruffles the branches of a pear tree. A girl in a short pink spring dress walks across the street. The sky is blue, cloudless, and harmless. So far. If his dad is right, L.A. will never look as peaceful as it does right now, ever again.

MINUS 7 HOURS: **San Diego; Greg**

Greg is driving to Costco to buy the biggest bags of rice, beans, and potatoes they have. He pictures his sister and mother sitting in Palm Springs at their kitchen table next to the patio with the swimming pool, with the air conditioner on, even though it's only March. His 80-year-old mother Inge is probably cutting coupons or studying baking recipes. How is he going to get through to them? No time to waste, just do it. His sister picks up.

"Rose, it's Greg."

"Oh hi, little brother. How nice to hear your voice? How is it going in beautiful San Diego? Is the weather pleasant and cool? We're already roasting here."

"I don't have time to chat. Can you put Mom on speaker phone? We have something very important to tell you."

"How exciting! Is it about the boys? Is Daniel getting married to that cute girlfriend of his?"

"No, nobody is getting married. We need you to pack up your car, and drive up to our cabin with Mom, right away."

"But Mom and I have to go shopping for a little get-together with the girls—" Rose interrupts.

"Rose, stop. A disaster is going to strike in seven hours. You need to come to the ranch now to be safe."

"Oh, I think we're perfectly safe here, aren't we Mom?"

"What kind of disaster?" Inge asks.

"A giant solar storm causing a global blackout," Greg explains.

"But we can't just pack up and go! And I would never find your cabin on my own anyway," Rose protests.

"You have to. I'll give you detailed directions."

"But we invited six women for a Kaffeeklatsch this afternoon. We can't just cancel on such short notice."

"Rose, listen to me, the whole fucking world as we know it is coming to an end in seven hours!" Greg is getting exasperated with his sister's petty concerns.

"Language, Greg."

"Look Rose and Mom we're not trying to frighten you, but this is serious. Very serious. The boys are already on their way."

"Oh my God, what are you saying? What are we going to do? I'm hyperventilating!" Rose's voice sounds at the edge of hysteria.

"Just do exactly what we tell you."

"Rose, give me the phone. I'm writing down the directions." Inge is taking over.

"What about the dog? What about Midnight?" Rose cries.

"Bring the dog. But please don't dilly-dally," Greg concedes.

"Don't worry." Inge is going into disaster planning mode. "It's just like earthquake preparation. No electricity, so we'll bring flashlights, and a battery-powered radio. We'll close up the house and disconnect everything."

"You got it, Mom," Greg says.

"Greg, I'm not leaving! Are you out of your mind! You can't just call here and tell us what to do?" Rose whines.

"Don't forget extra clothes and practical shoes and whatever non-perishable food you have," Greg adds, ignoring Rose's outburst.

"Got it. Now give me those directions," Inge says.

"No, no, no!" Rose shouts.

Minus 6 hours: Vega

Greg turns to Vega. "Is there anything you cannot live without here?"

"I'm packing my Tibetan scroll painting of the goddess

Tara," she tells him. "It takes no space at all." The thangka of Tara is Vega's most meaningful item and has been with her since her early twenties when she found it in a small shop in Katmandu. Tara is the goddess of compassion, her body is sky blue, and she sits on a golden lotus throne, one hand extended outward in a wish-fulfilling gesture. Tara has been Vega's guide and protectress for decades. She could never part with it.

"Do we have all our important documents?" Greg asks.

"Already in the car. Family pictures?"

Vega opens the cabinet door and lets her hand glide across the backs of about a dozen family albums she has assembled, designed, and labeled since the birth of the boys. All those memories, the first steps, the birthdays, holidays in Europe—hard copy photos from before flash drives existed.

She slides down to the ground and opens one album at random. A picture of Stevie as a toddler, in the garden looking for Easter eggs. His round face framed by the white-blond hair in a delighted grin as he puts a yellow egg into his basket.

"I can't … leave all these behind," Vega whispers.

"You have to. We're only bringing the photos on the computer and on the flash drive. I know it's hard, but we have limited space, and maybe in a few days this is all over and we can come back." Greg is carrying bags of clothes and boxes of food to the car.

"Will the computer even work?"

"We won't have internet, but we have solar power and you can still look at pictures."

Vega's heart aches, but she nods. Considering the scale of this catastrophe, a few baby pictures are the least of their worries. She hears Stevie's heavy black combat boots stomp up to the front entrance, runs to the door and hugs her son, now almost a head taller than her. Through his black leather jacket, she feels his strong chest and muscled shoulders. He's been working out. Her youngest is not her baby anymore. At twenty-five, he is an independent young man who's forged a creative career in the film industry.

"I'm so glad you're here," she says into his shoulder, wanting to hold onto this hug a little longer.

"That was a $350 Uber ride," he says.

"No matter. After this solar storm you won't be able to use your credit card anyway," Greg says.

"Grab one thing you really can't live without."

"Jeez, this all sounds so final."

"Maybe it is, and if not, then there's no harm done."

Stevie stomps into his old room and stuffs shirts and pants into his backpack. "I'm taking these." He holds up his two Japanese Katana swords. Makes sense.

"All right, let's go."

The Toyota SUV is stuffed to the brim with sacks of flour, rice, beans and four large cans of olive oil. One of the seats is down, to make space for bedding, clothes bags and the safe. It looks like one of the camping trips when the kids were small and she had to bring everything along.

As Vega locks up the house, her hands tremble. She has to sit down on the wooden stoop to calm her breathing. When will they return? And if they do, what will it look like? The solar storm cannot destroy the house, but people can. This house holds half a lifetime of memories, milestones, celebrations, and losses. She looks around her garden, her blooming purple Jacaranda tree, her herbs. All the plants she has planted, nurtured, and taken care of over the years. "Can I bring my tomato plant?"

"There's no space." Greg waves the car keys in the air.

"I'll hold it on my lap."

MINUS 5 HOURS: **Vega**

At 5 p.m., the eastbound I-8 freeway is sluggish with rush hour traffic. Vega looks at the people in their cars, driving home from work, stressed about sitting in traffic. What is going to happen to them? What will their world look like tomorrow? She holds on to her tomato plant, as if it were her life preserver.

Stevie in the backseat is in his own world is swaying to music. Greg has turned on the radio. A news report announces a minor solar flare, which could cause "sporadic" power outages.

"I can't believe they aren't giving people any warning," Stevie says.

"I was just thinking the same thing."

"Rakesh told me this classified information in confidence. He and I could be criminally liable if we pass this on," Greg tries to explain.

"Some could escape, like we are." A wave of guilt washes through Vega's gut for escaping and leaving all these people behind.

"Only if they have an off-grid place like us."

"Everything else gets fried?"

"Powerlines will melt, and transformers explode. Televisions, cable boxes, cell phones, computers, radios thermostats, electric stoves—ruined beyond repair, if the solar storm is strong enough," Stevie says from the back seat.

"Rakesh said G5."

"That's the highest level. Only electronic devices protected in a metal box and turned off during the ejection can survive."

"How do you know so much about this, Stevie?"

"Post-apocalyptic fiction. It's a popular genre in my generation. But Daniel is the real expert."

"Let's hope our solar system inside the garage at the cabin will survive. It has a meal roof and metal siding. That's our best chance."

It feels like a punch to Vega's stomach. She should open the window and scream out a warning to all the unsuspecting souls.

Instead, she watches office buildings go by. Soon they are replaced by suburban shopping malls. As they keep driving the scenery turns more rural; there's space between buildings; they are interspersed with orchards and wooded hills. Orange wildflowers have sprung up on the shoulders of the freeway. The mountains loom in the distance. El Cajon Mountain in the El Capitan County Preserve the leader of them, a mid-sized mountain range with a crooked back like an old horse.

"Do you want to listen to music?" Stevie offers from the back seat.

She turns off the radio. Might as well.

To the tunes of the *Grateful Dead,* they pass the turnoff for Alpine and cross underneath a freeway overpass. On the other side civilization falls away. Usually at this part of the drive, she breathes a little deeper. No more buildings, just rolling hills and canyons, strewn with large boulders as far as the eye can see. The hills are green from the recent rains. There are still a lot of bare trees, with only a hint of light green on some branches this early in the year. Can a solar storm cause a wildfire? Vega doesn't know what will happen. The future is a blank slate of possibilities—most of them terrifying.

They exit the freeway onto the winding country road CA 79 toward Cuyamaca Lake. Driving through the small village of Descanso with its trading post, saloon, and antique stores, Vega sees a few men with cowboy hats inside the saloon, drinking beer. Would it be better if they knew what was coming, or is ignorance bliss?

"Greg, we should be warning our friends at least!"

"Vega, I know how you feel. I don't agree with this government decision, but I have to protect Rakesh. He told me in confidence, even though it was government classified information. He said, get your family out of here. And we did. That's all we can do right now."

"I'm calling Mina. She's one of our oldest friends."

Greg's jaw sets in a grim, tense line. He shakes his head, but Vega is already on her phone.

"Mina? Listen, you need to get out of town. A terrible solar storm is going to hit earth tonight. It's going to destroy the electric grid. I'm putting you on speaker-phone. I'm in the car with Stevie and Greg. We're on our way to our mountain cabin."

"What are you talking about? There's nothing in the news and where would we go?" Mina's voice comes over of the speakerphone.

"They're not announcing it, that's why I'm calling you."

"Vega, you sound hysterical. I don't know what you're trying to do, but don't mess with me and try to frighten us."

"At least prepare ..."

The line goes dead. Vega looks at Greg.

"She hung up on me. She didn't believe me," Vega says.

Greg nods.

At the end of the village, the traffic stops. Cars line up bumper to bumper. A group of locals have occupied the road and are marching in a circle holding up protest signs.

Vega's heart stops. Did they find out and are demonstrating about the government's lack of warning and preparation? Greg rolls down the window. They strain to hear what they are shouting.

Stevie has the best eyes and ears. "*No More Power Shut Offs,*" he reads out loud.

"They found out," Vega says. "They are protesting about the solar storm."

"No," Greg corrects her. "The local power company has been turning off the power here during Santa Ana winds to prevent forest fires. Shutting off the electricity during a solar storm would actually be a good thing."

"Oh no," Vega feels anxiety rise in her stomach. Her mouth gets dry, and her heart starts to race. "They're protesting about the wrong thing, and we can't get through the only road." *What if we won't make it to the ranch in time and can't disconnect the solar system? What if we are stuck here in limbo, and then in chaos?*

"Yeah, we can't afford to sit here in traffic for long," Greg looks at Vega and apparently noticed how pale she has turned. "We still have four hours."

"Relax, Mom the sheriff is letting cars through up ahead," Stevie notices.

A deputy guides them on the road's shoulder past the

demonstrators. Vega rolls down her window and shouts at the protesters "Turn off the power. It's the right thing to do!"

"What do you know, lady!" a protester shouts back angrily.

Vega swallows hard.

"Keep quiet, at least for Rakesh's sake," Greg hisses.

They turn left into a smaller road winding uphill through forests and meadows, where cows graze peacefully in the evening sun. A few fruit trees show the first tentative flower buds. As the car climbs higher in altitude, pine and oaks trees line the road. Timid light green tips of leaves try to break through. Every turn reveals a new vista, a new outlook. An ancient oak tree reaches its branches into the sky, its battered trunk scarred by lightning.

They drive through a green tunnel of live oak trees, through speckled sunlight, before the landscape opens up onto a wide meadow where deer graze in the shadows of sugar pines. At Middle Peak, the road rounds along the lake, which lies glittering and still in the evening light. Up here, none of the city's frenzy seems to matter.

Another turn-off onto the narrow one-lane Sugar Pine Road, past the fire station. On the other side of the crest the entire county, all the way to the ocean is spread out in front of her. The golden reflection off the sea in the far distance shimmers like a pool of gold. She stares in silence. Almost there. A few more turns, the trees are getting thicker and the shade deeper. Here a few daffodils dot the slope, before they come to the final turn off onto the dirt lane leading to the cabin.

Greg slows down and shifts into four-wheel drive to navigate the pitted path. They climb one last hill, and the ranch is lying before them on the ridge of Kosmik Peak. The large garage—the size of a barn—sits next to the dirt road. Down the steep, paved driveway they go, to the gray house, built into the hillside above Shelter Valley and opening toward the distant sea in the west. Vega takes a deep breath and, as always when she comes here, she feels calmer.

Daniel's Tesla and Rose's Volvo station wagon are already parked in the driveway. Daniel is carrying boxes into the house. Rose is helping Inge out of the car. A black-haired man stands next to Rose and a young girl Vega has never seen before is running down the hill with Midnight, who's sniffing every rock and tree trunk delighted with all the new smells.

MINUS 3 HOURS: **Vega**

The sun is just about to set over the ocean. Deep orange, it hovers over the cloud bank, stretching from El Cajon Mountain to San Clemente Island and San Jacinto Mountains in the north. Vega watches it sink, slowly, gracefully behind the marine layer enveloping the coastline in the west.

This same benevolent sun has gilded the hilltops every sunset. But tonight, it will explode into fiery flares and threaten an entire civilization? Vega can't fathom it. It hasn't sunk in, and she hopes this may be just another false alarm about the end of the world like Y2K.

Vega hugs Daniel, Lin, and Inge, but who is the girl and the dark-skinned man with the mustache? Rose introduces him as her boyfriend, Tarek, and his daughter, Eleni. It's news to Vega that Rose has a boyfriend.

Greg's face darkens at the sight of these two strangers.

"How do you know my sister Rose?" he asks the man.

"We met through an online dating service two weeks ago," the man called Tarek says with a slight accent.

"Tarek is an engineer," Rose says proudly as if this that would explain everything, "He's also a single dad to his twelve-year-old daughter Eleni." She squeezes Tarek's arm and pushes her peroxide blonde hair behind her ear.

"Why are we here?" Tarek asks.

"I'll explain later," Greg says with barely concealed hostility.

Vega can feel his irritation.

"No, I need to know now!" Tarek insists. "I left my work at the desalination plant when Rose told me it was a matter of life and death that I come with her. I can't afford to lose my job."

A moment of silent stand-off follows. A crow flies overhead and caws. They are still standing in the cabin's driveway, luggage and supply sacks piled at their feet. It's the twilight time between day and night. Vega senses that Greg is about to explode. Not a good beginning for a forced co-habitation with this stranger plus daughter. Not a good beginning for gaining trust.

"You are welcome to go back," Greg says with barely contained anger.

"No, Tarek. You must stay!" Rose pleads, clinging to his arm. "I couldn't just leave him and his daughter behind. If it's really as dangerous as Greg says, I had to get them out of harm's way!"

Tarek squeezes Rose's hand.

"I made it very clear. Only family!" Greg hisses.

"You just don't want me to be happy!" Rose whines. "I haven't been in a relationship in years!"

Vega rolls her eyes. Rose always was a drama queen. Tarek's daughter is playing with Midnight, and Daniel is bringing luggage and supplies into the house. He flashes a glance at Greg. Daniel brought his girlfriend, Lin. Three non-family-members. They can't turn them away. They'll just have to accommodate them. What else is there to do? At least she knows Lin, who has a good head on her shoulders, but what kind of a person is Tarek?

"I will not wait any longer!" Tarek demands and Rose nods her head vigorously. "We drop everything and take Eleni out of school and now you won't even give us an explanation. Enough already. We want to know what's going on *now!*" Tarek's face turns red as he raises his voice.

Oh, he's that kind of person, Vega thinks. A bit volatile

Greg drops the sack of rice he hoisted. Everybody gathers around. Will he explode or will he explain?

He takes a big breath to stay calm "I have credible reason to believe that tonight in about three hours, a CME — a coronal mass ejection or a giant solar storm— will erupt and bombard the earth's atmosphere with powerful gamma rays, disrupting the electromagnetic field and disabling all electric and digital devices indefinitely."

"What does that mean?" Rose is not satisfied.

"Couldn't we just turn off our electric devices at home?" Tarek asks.

"Because you can't reconnect them. They'll be fried. Here we run on solar power, we're not connected to the grid. We can disconnect our battery tonight, and then hopefully reconnect it tomorrow morning."

"Do you know the size of the CME?" Daniel asks.

"My source said 'the biggest since the Carrington event,' whatever that means."

"The Carrington event in 1859 was the most intense G5 geomagnetic storm in recorded history. A CME of this magnitude today will cause catastrophic black outs. Not good," Daniel explains.

Rose frowns but seems temporarily placated. Tarek seems to grasp the situation and nods. "In that case, thanks for giving us shelter," he says and grabs a bag of groceries to carry into the house.

Vega looks at Greg, who shakes his head in exasperation. They continue to carry sacks of rice, beans, oatmeal, and large cans of olive oil down to the basement for storage. Vega stocks the shelves of the big refrigerator with frozen food, milk, butter, cheeses, and anything else people have brought from home. The food should last through the night, while the fridge is disconnected. She places the canned goods and dry supplies on the shelves Greg installed for his growing wine cellar.

Inge helps Vega make a big pot of stew, with chicken, potatoes, and perishable vegetables.

Minus 2 hours: **Vega**

Nine people sit around the table eating bowls of stew. It's the first time since this morning that Vega has stopped running, that she actually stopped to sit down and think. Every face looks drawn and anxious.

"Thank you for trusting me enough to drop everything and get here so quickly," Greg begins. His eyes linger on Tarek, whom he didn't invite. "I didn't ask you lightly. If my information is correct—and I have all the reason to believe it is—we will wake up in a very different world tomorrow. A world without electricity, without computers, without cars, without electric light or appliances."

All eyes are on Greg.

"After dinner," Greg continues, "we will turn off our electric solar system and disconnect our lithium-ion battery to prevent it from being shorted. Hopefully, we can turn it back on tomorrow when the solar storm is over. Until then we have candles and flashlights. We all should try to get some sleep. It's been a crazy day. Any questions?"

"Why isn't anybody else leaving? Why isn't there a warning on the radio or TV?" Rose wants to know.

"A friend in the government risked his job to warn me. It's classified information and under the threat of criminal liability. He said I could only tell my immediate family," Greg says pointedly, looking at Tarek. Rose doesn't seem to notice.

"What about all the other people? What will happen to them?" Inge asks.

She echoes Vega's thoughts. With a hard clump of anxiety in the middle of her stomach, the faces of their friends and neighbors pass through her mind. What will happen to them?"

"Good question. I don't know. I believe the government is trying to prevent riots and mass hysteria."

"Won't that happen anyway, if this solar storm really hits?" Stevie asks.

"Probably." Greg agrees.

He clearly doesn't want to go there, Vega thinks. He was always good at compartmentalizing problems and dealing with the most pressing priorities first.

"Are you a prepper? Did you expect this disaster? How come you are so prepared?" Tarek asks.

"We just built this cabin here for a peaceful place away from the city. We did not anticipate an apocalypse. We only found out today, Tarek." Vega says in a soothing voice, trying to calm down her sister-in-law's boyfriend.

"A total collapse of the electric grid was going to happen soon anyway," Daniel interjects. "With global warming, the power grid is getting more and more strained from all the air conditioners and would have shut down at the next big heat wave."

"That's a relief," Rose says sarcastically. "How long will we have to stay here?

"Couldn't everyone just shut off their cell phones, computers?" Tarek asks.

"The surge of electrons will be so powerful, it will destroy electronic parts whether they are turned off or not," Daniel explains. "Hopefully, the metal roof and siding of our garage will serve as a Faraday's cage and protect the solar battery and system inside."

"What's a Faraday cage?" Rose asks.

"It's an enclosure made of conductive materials such as metal used to guide electromagnetic fields along its surface to the ground, protecting what's inside," Daniel explains. "Turn off your cellphones and computers and put them into this metal box, and we will store it in the garage until tomorrow."

"We can still listen to downloaded music, can't we?" Stevie is the music expert in the family.

"Good point. Throw in the Wonderboom speaker as well."

Everybody around the table throws their cell phone

into a metal toolbox. It's obvious from their expression that no one wants to part with their devices. When Vega adds her cell phone to the pile, even she feels somehow naked without it.

"Any other electronics?" Greg asks.

"My Apple watch?" Inge asks with trepidation.

"Absolutely. Microprocessors are very vulnerable to fluctuations in power. They don't stand a chance."

Inge hands over her watch to Daniel, who adds it to the pile.

"I'm not giving up my cell phone," Tarek declares.

"Fine. Suit yourself." Greg's patience is obviously stretched to the breaking point.

Let him keep his cell phone, Vega thinks. He won't be able to use it anyway after tonight.

"Can we go to the bathroom and brush our teeth?" Rose asks.

"Yes. Our water service won't be disrupted. Our water system runs on gravity, not electricity. We have our own well and cistern."

"How long will the power be out?" Inge has been very quiet all evening.

"Two years, at least." Daniel says in a low voice.

"Two years?" Rose shouts. Others gasp in dismay and disbelief.

"However—there is one amazing side effect to this solar storm," Daniel tries to interrupt the outburst.

They all look at him. "A silver lining?" Rose asks.

He nods. "When the gamma rays hit the earth's atmosphere, the CME should cause a global aurora borealis like the Northern Lights. In about three hours, an incredible light show will illuminate the night sky."

"What does that mean?" Vega asks.

"Nobody knows for sure, but it should be a fantastic, cosmic spectacle."

Minus 1 hours: **Vega**

It is getting late, and everybody is exhausted. Inge and Rose are washing the dishes. The only sounds interrupting the tense silence is the clinking of the silverware and the clatter of the ceramic bowls as they place them in the drying rack. Vega is pacing back and forth in front of the large picture window looking out over the valley. But there is only a black, moonless sky with pinpricks of stars.

"It's almost time," Greg says and goes to the garage with Daniel to turn off the solar converter. The rest of the family sit around the table, not sure how to spend the last few minutes before the apocalypse. Greg and Daniel return and join them.

"It's happening!" Vega exclaims. The lights go out and the far horizon—where she can normally see the city lights in the far distance, San Diego directly west, Oceanside and Ramona toward the Northwest, and the hazy glow of Los Angeles over the mountains in the north— has turned black, pure darkness, except for bright flashes right where the skyline of San Diego should be. A fiery flash descends and crashes into the horizon. Another one, further south, and then another north of Oceanside, and more and more, some brighter, others faint, as if from a long distance. *Shock and awe,* Vega thinks, like the terrifying fireworks at night during the invasion of Iraq. "What is it?" Vega whispers.

"Those are the planes, falling from the sky," Daniel says, "as their propulsion systems fail."

Another faint explosion toward the north over LA makes Vega shiver. She sends a silent prayer for all the lives lost this moment.

O HOURS: **Vega**

They all turn to the giant picture window, which takes up the entire length of the house and captures the expanse of the night sky.

Now the real light show begins. Swirls of green and yellow veils roll across the sky. They turn over like waves, changing colors to purple and blue, evolving, expanding, enlarging, erasing the stars. Like a river of light, the swirls flow toward them, reaching beyond and above the mountain into space, forming cascades, pillars of light, merging, coalescing. A tongue of green light flashes across their field of vision. Fingers of florescent turquoise spread out as if to touch and reach every corner of the universe. Like wisps of a rainbow, they change direction and recede overhead.

Eleni lets out a short cry. Tarek holds her in his arms and strokes her back. Midnight whimpers. Inge and Rose turn around the dining chairs and watch from first row seats. Daniel and Lin stand hand in hand. Greg has put his arm around Vega, who trembles in awe and terror at the grandeur and beauty of this cosmic display.

A waterfall of fire rains down onto the valley in undulating moving streams of green and purple. Giant fingers of green fire seem to stretch and reach toward their cabin. Vega grasps Greg's arm convinced the fiery fingers in the sky will reach them and burn them. Now! She never imagined the apocalypse, but this is what it would look like. She turns to Stevie, standing by himself and touches his arm. He looks at her with tears streaming down his face. Vega folds him into a hug.

If this is the last thing I ever see, it's not a bad way to go out.

2

DAY 1: GREG

We're still alive. Rakesh was right. The sun is rising over the mountains in the east, harmlessly, as if nothing had happened. As if it hadn't caused a light show of biblical proportions only a few hours ago. Thirty minutes and it was all over. Just like Fourth of July fireworks. The lights dissolved. The night sky reappeared, studded with pale stars smudged at the edges with the approaching dawn. What they had witnessed was too large for words, so they shuffled back to their beds silently. Each processing in their own way what they had seen.

Greg is the first one up, as usual, and he makes his way up to the garage in the pale morning light to reconnect the solar batteries. Dew coats the rosemary bush and the blooming mountain lilac shrub. The air feels fresh, and birds are twittering like any other day. But this won't be a normal day. Will anything ever be normal again?

In the garage the solar inverters start humming right away, as they are supposed to. The batteries are charged. Since they are not connected to the global electric grid, and the system is protected by the metal cage of the garage, the system didn't get shorted out by the solar storm. Good. He can make coffee. A lot of coffee.

Daniel joins Greg to check on the cars. Daniel's Tesla is ruined.

"The low voltage, microscopic layout of its microprocessor-controlled devices, is extremely vulnerable to the slightest fluctuation in power. It didn't have a chance against the rising amperage," Daniel says with resignation. His Tesla was his pride and joy.

"Maybe the Toyota RAV survived." Greg is hopeful. The SUV was inside the metal garage. He tries to start the engine. Nothing. Just silence.

"It was too new, too sensitive. I guess we'll be walking from now on."

Daniel nods miserably.

"One thing at a time. Coffee first, then we'll see what's next." Greg tries to cheer him up. But Daniel doesn't drink coffee.

BACK IN THE CABIN, Daniel is fiddling with a battery-powered transistor radio they brought back from the garage. Only one announcement is broadcasting from all stations:

"This is the emergency broadcast system. We have experienced a Coronal Mass Ejection or solar storm of global proportions. All electric systems have been disabled. Please remain in your homes. The streets are unsafe and gasoline pumps are not functioning. Boil water before consumption. We are in the process of setting up relief and supply stations. We ask for your patience. We will update the public as new information becomes available."

The announcement is followed by the emergency sound he's heard so often during the tests, which used to interrupt the regular programming. Then the announcement begins again.

"This is the emergency broadcast system ..."

"You can turn it off, Daniel. We'll check for updates later. Let's save the battery." Greg wonders how are people supposed to boil the water without gas or electricity? "It will be a while before we get any real information." Greg tells him.

Daniel turns off the radio. "I remember how long it took for the government to bring aid to New Orleans after Katrina hit, and that was without a global black out."

"How are they even broadcasting at all?" Lin asks.

"The emergency broadcast system runs on generators. I assume the government had them in a protected space.

Otherwise, back-up generators will fail. It's only one channel, one frequency," Daniel explains.

"At least our solar battery works. We'll have power for the refrigerator, and the hot water heater." Greg says from the kitchen area, as he turns on the faucet and water pours out. So far so good. He fills the glass pot of the coffee maker to the rim and puts it in the coffee machine. He fills the grinder with coffee beans and pushes the 'on' button. Nothing happens. Of course, the electrical parts have been fried. They should have moved the coffee machine and the coffee grinder into the garage with the rest of the electronics. With nostalgia, he remembers his grandmother's hand-turned coffee grinder with the handle on top. Greg turns on the gas stove, but the ignition system is gone. He tries the lighter. No go. Matches finally light the flame for the water kettle. They'll have to drink tea.

Tarek looks over Greg's shoulder. "Let me work on it. I'll figure out a way to grind the coffee. It could be worse."

"It is worse," Rose says from the door of the guest room, where they slept with Eleni, who has a mattress on the floor. "There's no hot water."

We're alive, Greg thinks, *but it won't be easy.*

BREAKFAST CONSISTS of tea with milk, toast with butter and jam, and scrambled eggs. The milk won't even last a week, thinks Greg. *The other items we'll use up within days.* Greg looks around the crowded table. The family and friends look relieved, exhausted, confused. He decides to give them a day to settle in, get acclimated, find their way around the property, and figure out where everybody is sleeping before he has to address the two major issues: security and supplies.

His glance rests on Tarek, the total stranger in his house, and his daughter Eleni, who sits with eyes cast down, eating. Did it just occur to him where he is? What his presence means for everybody? How could his sister bring him here after knowing him for only two weeks? And his daughter. Two more mouths to feed. Two more people needing a bed. Two more people to integrate into their family.

As if reading his thoughts, Tarek looks up and meets Greg's eyes. "I'll work on the hot water heater and the coffee grinder," he says.

Greg nods. How can he trust this man? It's survival of the fittest, and they are vulnerable.

3

DAY 3: VEGA

Vega wakes up early. While everybody sleeps, she hangs up the scroll painting of the blue Tara on her bedroom wall. She needs the goddess now more than ever. Her smile and her calming hand gestures hold pink lotus flowers. She helps Vega to feel more grounded and prepared to deal with the coming uncertainty.

She climbs up Kosmik Peak to watch the sunrise over Volcan Mountain in the east. The pink light spreads out over Shelter Valley, one slope at a time, leaving some in cool shade, while bathing other meadows and groves in warming morning rays.

She wants to remind herself why they came here in the first place. Why she and Greg built a home into the hillside, carving out a place from the rocky slope to perch above the valley and above the hills stretching all the way to the coast in the west. They wanted to stay above petty politics and get away from small-minded jealousies and rivalries. They wanted to get away from disease and infections. They wanted to keep the big picture in mind, to stay in touch with the rhythm of the four seasons, the changing nature of shrub oak and sugar pine, the wild turkeys and shy deer visiting daily at twilight. *A place above the fray. But the fray has caught up with us.*

She wonders where Tarek and his daughter came from. Their accent sounds Middle Eastern, but she can't be sure. How did they get here? What is their story? Eleni is so young, but at least she is safe with them, for now.

When she gets back to the cabin, everybody is assembled around the table finishing breakfast. Greg announces that he is installing a security system with Tarek and Stevie, while Daniel will monitor the radio broadcasts for updates. *Greg's like a general, assigning tasks to his troops,* Vega thinks.

"We'll make another stew out of the remaining perishable vegetables and meats for tonight," Vega says.

"Let's take an inventory of our supplies and freeze whatever we can." Inge is good at making lists. Fortunately, the fridge downstairs in the basement survived the solar storm. The basement is built into the mountain, and the insulation protected the fridge's electric parts.

"Absolutely," Vega agrees. "Then we can make a menu

plan how to use most efficiently what we have and determine how long our supplies will last."

GREG:

Tarek finds a spool of electrical cable and an old, red bicycle light in a dusty corner of the garage. He wipes off the cobwebs and holds the light up for Greg to see. "I can rig this up as an alarm."

"Sure, you're the engineer. Could you connect it to the fire alarm bell, in case an intruder approaches at night?"

"We need a motion sensor," Tarek says. Greg is moderately impressed with Tarek. He seems to be able to work with the supplies at hand. He managed to repair a short in the water heater, which was partially protected from the solar flare by a metal box. No luck with the coffee grinder though.

"What kind of job did you do before coming here?"

"My company services the San Diego water treatment plants. I'm a trouble shooter," Tarek says, not without pride.

No wonder he's so good at improvising. "I imagine a lot can go wrong in a water treatment plant." Greg tries to be subtle in learning more about Tarek, without being too obvious.

"I was part of a team building water treatment plants in my home country. We worked under much harder conditions than here." Tarek is searching through a box with mechanical bits and pieces in the garage.

"What is your home country?" Stevie is sitting on a rusty paint can, waiting for instructions.

"Syria," Tarek says and straightens. "Eleni and I are from Aleppo."

"When did you leave?" Greg has seen the pictures of the destroyed city of Aleppo in the news.

"We were evacuated in 2013," Tarek says in a toneless voice.

Greg conjures the new images from this horrible event, when civilians were stranded in the streets of the besieged city in the cold nights of early April, while Russian and Syrian government forces attacked and disrupted the evacuation routes of the Red Crescent.

"Eleni and I were some of the last ones who made it out." Tarek's voice has dipped to barely a whisper.

"I'm so sorry." Greg feels his resentment against this intruder on their family shrink, as he pictures Tarek and Eleni's narrow escape.

"Nice. You have a motion sensor light in here," Tarek announces, clearly eager to change the subject. "I can connect it to the bicycle light and the fire bell."

"Good." Greg had forgotten about the light. Together they unroll the cable up the hill to the highest point on the dirt road, where Tarek attaches it to a sugar pine tree. Stevie is trailing behind.

"How are we going to avoid a deer setting off the

alarm?" Stevie asks and imitates a deer standing wide-eyed in the middle of the road while the alarm goes off.

"We'll let you figure out the height, Stevie," Greg decides. "A little higher than a deer, but not too high for a car."

While Stevie measure heights on the tree trunk, Tarek and Greg dig a shallow ditch to bury the cable. It will connect it to the solar batteries in the garage.

"I still can't believe this is happening, that my job, my life in the outside world is basically over. It just hasn't sunk in yet. I almost didn't come. I didn't believe it was real. But Rose insisted and I couldn't let her down," Tarek says to Greg.

"I know it feels unreal. But you've heard the emergency broadcast system. Unless they have generators or solar batteries that were protected in a metal structure, people are without power. And without water. We have to prepare and be ready for desperate people coming to get what we have here."

"I still feel I should go back to work. My job is very important to me. I feel fortunate that I got it, that I'm not just another unemployed refugee. I'm good at it and can't just let that go." Tarek lays another piece of cable and covers it carefully with dirt.

"You're an engineer, Tarek. You can get a job anywhere," Greg uncoils more cable.

"It's not easy for me to be accepted and respected at work."

Greg doesn't answer. Of course, he has no idea what it's like to fight for every bit of recognition. Surely Tarek had to overcome doubts in his abilities every day. Greg has his own company and he's lily white. Everyone respects him. No questions asked.

"Eleni and I are two more mouths to feed. How long can we last on the food supplies?"

Good question, Greg thinks. *What can you contribute, Tarek, besides laying cable?*

"If we're lucky, we can last a month. We'll have to supplement by hunting and growing our own food." Greg digs the next part of the ditch and unravels another section of electric cable from the spool.

"I don't know how to hunt. Do you have weapons? And what about Eleni's schooling?"

We have to deal with his daughter too.

"We'll all have to learn new skills. Rose used to be a teacher. She can establish a routine and make sure Eleni keeps up with her reading and math. There's nothing for you back in the city."

"Yeah, I guess," Tarek rubs his back.

"Hey, Stevie, have you figured out where to attach the motion detector light? I've got some wire to tie it to the trunk," Greg calls to his son.

"Okay, Dad, but now I'm worried about squirrels climbing up the tree and checking out our sensor."

"We'll take that chance," Greg says, much to the disappointment of Stevie.

"All we need now is a test. Stevie, you can be our intruder," Greg says after the cable has been connected.

"Gladly." Stevie jumps up and down in front of the sensor while making horrifying noises.

Tarek waves from the front door. "The light is blinking inside."

Thirty seconds pass, then the fire alarm rings with frightening intensity.

Rose, Vega, and Inge rush to the door.

"What is that racket all about?" Rose asks.

"It's our new alarm system. In case of intruders. It works," Tarek says and smiles at Rose.

"So, what are we supposed to do if an intruder approaches?" Rose challenges him, fists clenched on her hips.

"Well," Tarek stammers, "that's something we need to discuss. Hey, Eleni," he changes the topic as he walks into the house. "What are you doing?"

Eleni is sprawled on the floor with Midnight. She has put her arms around the dog's neck and rests her head on his furry body. Tarek joins her. Together they stroke Midnight, who loves the attention.

"When can I go back to school?" Eleni asks.

Tarek meets Greg's eye and bites his lower lip. "We're going to homeschool you for a while, Rose and I. We're just getting organized. We're going to stay here for a bit, with Greg and Vega. You want to read a book together?"

Eleni nods.

"Let's go outside and sit on a blanket under the trees. Midnight can come too."

Not a lot of books to choose from. Greg watches Tarek browse through their book collection in the cabin. Esoteric texts on Tibetan Buddhist Art and a practical guide to beekeeping. These extra guests have a lot of special needs. They'll just have to cope with the situation, if they want to stay. And that's not a done deal yet in Greg's mind. Who knows what Tarek is capable of?

4

DAY 7: VEGA

With her hands in the soapy water of the sink, Vega looks at the pile of dirty dishes still cluttering every surface of the kitchen. Nobody is around to help. They all disappeared after breakfast, which is not an easy feat in the small cabin. She has swept up the crumbs on the floor and carried the cups from the table to the sink.

Vega looks out the window over the sink, up at the driveway and the hill leading up to the dirt road. A deer grazes peacefully on the grass and a second one looks down at her. They lock eyes. For a moment time stands still, as the sun reflects off the light green leaves of the oak tree. A breeze ruffles the deer's fur and they both trot off into the brush. Vega sighs. Probably everybody is outside to enjoy the sunshine. She tackles the first bowl and puts it into the drying rack after rinsing the soap off. At the fifth bowl, Daniel appears.

"Mom, we are out of toilet paper," he announces.

"Well, that was bound to happen. Can you help me here?"

"Sure," he dries one of the bowls, "But what about ..."

"We'll just have to use leaves, I suppose. Or water, that's how they do it in India."

"Yikes. We are also out of bread." He dries each dish as Vega loads it into the rack.

"We'll have to eat rice and beans and oatmeal. At least we have plenty of that."

"Okay, but what about the trash?"

"Your dad and Stevie are digging a big hole out back behind the garage. We'll burn as much as we can and bury the rest. With time, we'll have less and less trash, as we run out of packaging material."

Daniel swallows hard. Vega wants to console him. At least they have food, at least they have water, they are together. She hates to think about the situation of most people in the outside world.

Eleni comes in, Midnight trailing her. The two of them are inseparable.

"I'm hungry." The girl pulls at Vega's shirt.

"Let's see what we have." Vega opens a drawer and surveys the content. After seven days their supply is dwindling.

"Can I have a peanut butter and jelly sandwich?"

They have flour for baking, but no yeast.

"How about some peanut crackers?" Vega pulls out a box of Wheat Thins and spreads peanut butter on the crackers. She sighs. It's the last box and the last jar of peanut butter.

STEVIE:

In the dim basement, Stevie counts the sacks of rice, beans, and cans of oil. Eight twenty-pound sacks of rice, six bags of beans, and five cans of oil. How long will it last? Maybe a couple of months. Barely.

He's hungry. He's hungry every day. At twenty-five, he is done growing, but he has a high metabolism and he's used to eating whenever and whatever he wants. With pangs of regrets, he thinks of the many times he ran to Chipotle and stuffed his face with burritos, often not even finishing the entire meal. Or the frequent Grub Hub orders, when he threw the copious leftovers in the garbage. His stomach growls, remembering the juicy Cali-burritos with spicy sauce and shredded salad he used to eat almost every day.

Now, they have two rationed meals a day to preserve supplies; a breakfast of watery hot cereal, and an early dinner of rice and beans, sometimes supplemented by canned corn, or tomatoes from Vega's garden. Only Eleni gets a snack at lunchtime, granola bars or peanut butter on crackers.

His stomach makes a painful lurch at the thought of peanut butter. Stevie has never experienced scarcity, only knew about it from news reports on TV or movies about famine in Africa, or the hungry years during WWII. He could probably ask his Grandma Inge about it. She lived in Germany during the war. But the images of starving people never really penetrated his consciousness. Hunger was something that happened to other people far away.

Stevie rummages through the shelves of canned soups, canned tomatoes, canned peas on the basement walls. They are no good to him. Hidden behind rows of canned corn, he spots a bag of potato chips. He grabs it and tears it open with a satisfying crunch of paper. He stuffs the chips into his mouth by the fistful. Concealed by food supplies and Greg's building materials, he sits in a folding chair, hoping to stay undiscovered. It is shameful not to share, and he feels guilty, but he cannot stop.

5

DAY 10: STEVIE

Stevie's watching the sunrise over the mountain. He couldn't sleep on the hard ground of the loft in his parents' bedroom any longer. *I have no idea how mom does it. Dad is snoring like a bear!* The red bicycle light above the entrance door on the inside of the cabin flashes furiously. Nobody else notices. They're all still fast asleep Then the fire alarm goes off. The large electric bell on the outside of the garage makes such a racket that everybody in the cabin plus Midnight, the black Lab, startle awake.

Stevie's dad jumps out of bed and into his jeans. He grabs his Glock from under the mattress. Within seconds, he's out the door, followed by Stevie. Daniel staggers up from the basement, where he and Lin made their bedroom.

In the gray, pre-dawn light they move up the paved driveway to the dirt road, taking cover whenever possible. A movement from the left freezes them in place. Ten wild turkeys flutter across the driveway, agitated by the noise and the humans' erratic behavior.

"False alarm." Greg emerges from his crouched position behind a tree. "The turkeys triggered the alarm."

"I don't think so, Dad. Stay down. I set the sensor above the height of a deer or turkey." Stevie continues on the path. Greg raises his weapon.

Stevie's heart is hammering in his chest. What is going to await them at the cusp of the hill?

"Please don't shoot!" a thin, female voice pleads.

At the crest of the dirt path a bedraggled figure emerges. She's limping and stooped over from carrying a heavy leather shoulder bag. Her short white hair is tousled above the cashmere coat. Her hands are raised in surrender.

"Aunt Hilde?"

"It's me. After Stevie's call, I decided to come here. I didn't know where else to go. My car ran out of gas down by the lake. I had to walk the last three miles up this mountain."

Greg looks at Stevie with raised eyebrows. "You called her?" he mouths. Stevie shrugs and rushes to Hilde's side, takes the bag from her and gives her a big hug. She's his godmother. She's been kind to him all his life. He wasn't about to abandon her in this disaster. Hilde leans on his shoulder with a sigh of relief.

"You scared us to death, Aunt Hilde."

Supporting her frail figure, they lead her down to the cabin. She is exhausted, but her bright blue eyes under the short white hair still sparkle with curiosity. The whole family is watching from the door.

"How did you get here, you brave soul?" Vega rushes to her side.

"Did anybody follow you?" Greg asks.

"I was careful. You can't trust anybody. People are getting desperate to survive. I saw a man hitting a woman over the head for a bag of chips."

Stevie swallows guiltily.

"Come on in." Vega and Stevie help Hilde down the stairs to the entrance.

Installed on a chair, a cold glass of water in her hands, and relieved of her coat, Hilde brings news from the city.

"I couldn't stay any longer, life has become a nightmare. There's no radio, or TV, no lights, no refrigeration, you can't charge your phone or computer. The toilets don't flush. The gas station pumps don't work, neither do the ATMs. The stores are closed and empty, if you can even get in the door. Most stores are looted. The security systems on the garages or entrance gates are disabled. I had to pry my garage open by hand. I ran out of gas by the lake. Walking the last miles up here in the dark, I felt like I'd die if I had to take another step."

"What about local government or FEMA, are they sending aid?" Daniel wants to know.

"What aid?" Hilde asks in exasperation. "Where are they? What are they doing to help? We have no communication, no food. For all I know they're somewhere in a bunker in Washington. Meanwhile the water doesn't work, because the pumps have failed and there is no food. Nobody is helping us." Hilde's hand is shaking as she lifts the water glass to her lips.

"You're safe now. Take a shower and get some rest." Vega puts her arms around Hilde's trembling shoulders. "The solar panels are working. We have power and hot water."

"Hot water! How wonderful! Please don't send me away. I have nowhere else to go."

"Of course, you'll stay. You're like family. We'll find a place."

Rose's mouth has turned into a thin, bitter line. She's obviously not happy about this new arrival.

"I threw all the food I had into the trunk of my car."

"I'm amazed your car even started," Daniel says. "When the solar storm hit all computers, oxygen sensors, distributors and ignition system were wiped out."

Hilde gives him a sly smile. "My late husband's 1964 collector's Ford Mustang was built before electronic parts became common. It's all mechanical. And to think of all the times I bitched about that car taking up space in my garage."

"Brilliant!" Daniel gives her a hug. "We can retrieve the car and have a mode of transportation."

"Give us your keys. Stevie and I will get your car, before someone else takes it." Hilde hands Greg her car keys.

"What about gas?"

"There are enough stranded cars on the road. We can syphon off the gas into this canister!" Greg holds up a red gas canister and a piece of hose.

Hilde disappears into the bathroom to shower and change.

Rose hisses, "Who called her?"

"I did," Stevie admits.

"We don't have space or food for another person." Rose stands in all her impressive height of six feet in front of Stevie who's sitting on the floor and looks down at him accusingly.

"May I remind you that you brought *two* uninvited guests," Stevie shoots back.

"That's why resources are sparse, and we can't afford another person."

"You heard her, she brought food." He gets up to stand right in front of her.

"We just took an inventory and as it stands, our supplies will maybe last three weeks, if we are careful," Rose counters.

"Hey, hey, we'll work it out. Just settle down," Vega intervenes. "Let's find out what Hilde brought."

GREG AND STEVIE walk the three miles down to the lake. Two stranded cars stand right in the middle of Sugar Pine Road. Enough to fill their canister. At the turn off to Route 79, they see Hilde's red Ford Mustang parked by the lake. It is surrounded by a group of five men trying to unlock the doors with a coat hanger. Others bang against the windows with rocks to break in. Greg and Stevie run the last two hundred yards.

"Get away from our car," Greg shouts at them.

Stevie's heart rate goes up a few notches. The men outnumber them. They form a defensive line between the car and Stevie and his father, hollow eyed, wide stance, threatening posture, holding up metal wrenches and rocks. *How are we going to get to the car?*

One man in a grimy, red-checkered flannel shirt, holding a four-pronged lug wrench, takes a step in their direction. Instinctively, Stevie takes one step back. Greg holds his ground.

A film rolls out in Stevie's mind. Scavengers in rags coming at Mad Max with their improvised bayonets, sticks and knifes. What does he have to defend himself? Instinctively he holds up his arm to shield himself.

The man with the wrench lifts his weapon, and Stevie flinches. The man looks desperate, wild-eyed, grimy, like someone who doesn't have anything to lose.

"Guys, we don't want to hurt anybody," a man in a

Chargers jersey says in a calming voice and steps in between Greg and the attacker.

"Stay out of this, Tanner." The man with the lug wrench tries to push him out of the way.

Should he intervene or let his dad handle it?

"Just step away from the car." Greg calmly flashes his Glock and clicks the safety off.

They stare at each other in a standoff. This could go either way. Stevie feels sweat on his forehead and running down his back. He hopes they don't see or sense his fear.

The man lowers his wrench.

"Hey, how about giving us the car radio? You have a car, and we have nothing. We walked all the way up here from Santee. We have to provide for our families," Tanner with the greasy hair and blue Charger's jersey challenges.

Greg looks at him. "What would you even do with a car radio? There's no electricity."

"Take it to the Black Market in town. Exchange it for food."

"Fair enough." Greg hands the gun to Stevie to hold Tanner and the other refugees in check, as he approaches the car and opens the passenger door with the keys. He hands everything he finds inside to the man: two pillows, a folded blanket, two bags of chips, a box of granola bars, a sleeping bag, a precious 5-gallon water jug, a full metal water bottle, a raincoat and a folding chair and umbrella. From under the seat, he pulls out a first aid kit.

Stevie watches with a sinking feeling when Greg

hands the medical kit over. But then remembers they have a big one at the cabin.

Tanner distributes the supplies amongst his group. He holds up the water jug. "That's why we came to the lake. Can't live without water," he says and walks off.

Stevie sits down at the side of the road and lets out a huge sigh of relief.

"I feel sorry for the poor devils." Greg says.

"Yeah," Stevie says, watching them go with their meager bounty. "They had no idea what was coming. And this is only the beginning."

The banks of the lake look appalling. The campground is overflowing with survivors and trash. After only ten days, they are already living in squalor. Tents and camps are set up all along the shore. The campers use lake water for washing and cooking. Shirts and pants hang on branches and lines between trees to dry. Anglers line the edge of the lake fishing for trout, which will be depleted in a matter of days. Worse, Stevie can smell human waste backing up from the strained septic system by the bathrooms.

Greg fills the gas they brought into the tank of the Mustang so they can drive back to the cabin.

THEIR ARRIVAL IS GREETED by the whole family crowding around the red Mustang. New supplies are a big deal. The biggest deal. Stevie, always the dramatic filmmaker, makes a grand production of stepping around the car to the back. With a flourish he opens the trunk.

"Ta-da!"

The lid pops open. Everybody stares. Hilde cringes in the background. She knows what's inside. Gold labeled, expensive bottles of French champagne, smoked salmon — vacuum wrapped—caviar in small glass jars, and triangular wedges of fine French cheeses. A moment of stunned silence, then Stevie starts to laugh. Lin joins in.

"Veuve Clicquot, Bollinger, Dom Perignot, Moet & Chandon ...," she bursts out.

"How do you know so much about champagne?" Stevie asks.

"My parents owned a liquor store."

"What good is champagne and caviar? For ten hungry people?" Rose blurts out, exasperated.

"Are you kidding? I love San André cheese and smoked salmon," Daniel says.

"Calm down, everybody," Greg says, still laughing. "We'll keep one of the champagne bottles, and some salmon and cheese, but we'll take the rest to the Black Market the refugees told us about. We'll trade the bulk of this stuff for something..." He's searching for words, looks at Hilde, who's trying to hide and has blushed with embarrassment. "Something more substantial. At this point, it's quantity over quality."

6

DAY 12: STEVIE

Stevie and his Dad are driving the red Ford Mustang into town. Stevie smeared some dirt on the car to avoid too much attention and gain some mountain cred. But just driving a car at all is a big deal.

At the outskirts of town, the scope of what happened finally hits Stevie. An abandoned car sits in the middle of the road. They have to swerve around other cars that have been left in the street when the CME hit and disabled all their functions. Chevys, SUVs, and sedans have been stripped of anything of value—even their tires—in the two weeks since the CME. Main Street is empty, except for the trash. Plastic bags are floating in the air like flaccid jellyfish.

It's really happening. We've landed in a post-apocalyptic

movie. It looks like a scene from Mad Max or Book of Eli. Maybe it wasn't all a waste of time watching these movies obsessively. Maybe it was good preparation.

Slater's Food Store on Main Street is cordoned off with yellow crime scene tape. A mans scurried past the front door. They stop and Greg rolls down his window. "What happened here?" he asks.

"You from around here?" the man asks suspiciously.

"Yeah. We live close to the lake. We come here often."

"I think I've seen you before," the man acknowledges. "You knew José, the janitor?"

"Sure, nice guy."

"He was shot inside."

"No shit. Why? Who did that? José was harmless enough," Greg exclaims.

"The *Superior Bastards*," the man pronounces the name in a mocking voice, "looted the store, as if it was theirs to take. José got in the way. So, they just shot him."

"What about the sheriff? Did he arrest them?"

"Nope. They're still strutting around as if they own this place. I gotta be careful what I say, or else I'll be next."

"No worries. We heard there's a Black Market. Do you know where it is?"

"Behind the church. But be careful of those Bastards."

"Where'd they come from? What are they?"

"*Neo-Nazis*," the man mouths silently and puts his finger over his lips.

"Got it. You take care too."

"By the way, nice car," he says with a smile.

"The only one that still drives."

They turn left toward the church. Stevie remembers José, a big fellow with a friendly face, always cleaning, re-stacking the produce to make it look tidy. He can't believe he's dead, murdered so some Neo-Nazis could ransack the store.

They see the Black Market from three blocks away. Greg turns into a side street, out of sight of the market and parks the car.

"Can't be too careful," he says as they approach on foot.

People are milling around, bargaining, negotiating. It almost looks like a pre-solar-storm swap meet. Except for everyone's clothing. The clothes are grungy and have assumed a uniformly gray hue, a mixture of dust, dirt and sweat. Except at the lake, water is too precious to waste on washing clothes. Stevie realizes how lucky he is. At the cabin they have enough water, and his mom and Rose wash his clothes in a tub and then hang them on lines to dry.

"Okay Stevie, stay close. People may try to just take the stuff from us. Be careful. Keep it inside this bag."

The church parking lot is covered with booths and blankets where people display their goods for barter. Stevie sees watches, jewelry, medicine, film cameras, books, tools, and fancy clothes for sale. He would have coveted the GoPro camera under normal circumstances. Now it's worthless.

After only a couple of minutes the hierarchy of this system emerges. On the periphery of the market, a number of tall, bearded men in army fatigues survey the scene, but do not actively participate. Their weapons are clearly visible at their belts.

They stand right next to the deputy sheriff who is wearing his white Stetson hat. Relaxed, thumbs in his belt under his bulging belly, fingers touching the gun, holstered at his side. Nothing escapes his glance.

Stevie motions toward them with his chin. "I think that's them. The Bastards," he mumbles to his dad. Greg nods.

A local farmer offers seedlings of plants on a blanket.

"We would like a few seedlings. In exchange we can offer an assortment of cheeses, caviar, and bottles of champagne."

The farmer just laughs them off. "Bottles of champagne and caviar? You might as well eat and drink that yourself. Nobody needs those anymore."

"How about the brie and parmigiana cheeses for carrot seeds and a few seed potatoes?"

"You got a deal if you throw in five gallons of clean water."

"You turn down champagne and want drinking water instead?" Stevie's voice rises above the humdrum of the market.

"I can't make tea or hot cereal with champagne," the farmer answers.

"We don't have any drinking water here," Stevie says in frustration.

"It's a free market. If you don't like it, go somewhere else," the farmer answers calmly.

Before Greg can answer, one of the Bastards ambles over. "Is there a problem?" he asks.

"None of your business!" Stevie says. Greg puts a calming hand on his arm.

"You heard him. Go somewhere else," the Bastard says. Before Stevie can react, he feels a left hook to his jaw. Stevie stumbles backwards, stunned. The pain sears through his nose and jaw. He has never been hit before. He didn't see that coming. Greg catches him before he falls. Stevie braces himself for a new attack, raising his arms to shield his head, expecting another blow. His face flushes red with shame and anger.

"I'm sorry, he meant no offense." He hears his father's calm voice. Very unlike him to offering an apology.

The Bastard raises his eyebrow and lowers his fist. He grunts and kicks Stevie's shin a couple of times with his army boots. He grabs a bottle of champagne and the brie cheese. The sellers and buyers at the market have withdrawn into a wide circle around Stevie, Greg, and the Bastard. They watch the confrontation, silently, paralyzed with fear.

"Take this as a warning. Next time you won't get off so

easy." The Bastard ambles back to his comrades and the sheriff, who gives him a nod of approval.

Stevie moans.

"Let's go Stevie." Greg pulls him up and Stevie limps along as fast as he can.

"We can't let him get away with this," Stevie protests. "My jaw may be broken." Stevie is reeling from the humiliation and the pain. Everybody is staring at them and giving them a wide berth. Nobody wants to be guilty by association.

"You'll be fine. I'll check out your jaw when we are out of reach," Greg mumbles. Keeping his head down, Stevie walks between the stalls until they find a table loaded with books at the edge of the market. They exchange two champagne bottles for four third-grade Readers for Eleni. Greg chooses a gardening book, and Stevie grabs the Zombie Survival Guide, a favorite of his childhood. He needs a little refresher. Update his skills. Develop a defense strategy for their compound. At least they won't come home completely empty handed.

The merchant trading the books turns out to be the former bookstore owner in Juniper, Patrick McMannon. A gentleman with graying, longish hair, dressed in a tweet jacket and a tie. They introduce themselves.

"Oh, your wife is a writer of mysteries, isn't she? Vega Stern. She brought in some of her books and we sold them at the store—before the solar storm."

"That's my Mom," Stevie says.

"How are things here in town?" Greg asks.

"As you can see, we have a militia force patrolling our activities." Patrick speaks barely above a whisper.

"What about the sheriff? Isn't he keeping the Bastards under control?"

"No, unfortunately, they're as tight as Midas' fist. A match made in hell."

"I made an acquaintance with that fist today," Stevie rubs his hurting jaw. "You take care and enjoy that champagne. It's a good one."

"I know. Life's too short to drink cheap champagne. Especially now."

7

DAY 14: GREG

G reg's up early climbing Kosmik Peak at sunrise to patrol the area. In the two weeks since they arrived, it's become a habit. As a former police officer and security specialist he owns a firearm. What a strange word—as if an arm would turn into fire, which of course, in a way, it does. But is the weapon really an extension of a body? He can put it down and use his arms to hug his wife and children, to cook delicious meals with limited supplies, to nurture his family.

But here he is, holding onto the Glock in his parka pocket. It's the top performer in reliability and safety. And safety is his job. Safety is what this is all about. His peaceful mountain is under siege. The incident at the Black Market drove that home. More and more desperate intruders from the cities come to the countryside to escape hunger and deprivation—bringing both with them.

He has to keep the family safe—together with two friends, Lin and Hilde, and the two strangers. He didn't sign up to take responsibility for the two Syrian refugees. Then again, they're all refugees now. Supplies are dwindling rapidly. There are too many people to feed.

Rounding the last bend in the trail to the peak and overlook, he ducks underneath red-barked Manzanita branches. The path is strewn with rocks studded with shiny, black patches of obsidian, giving them the appearance of a leopard pattern. The spots look like round metallic burn marks. Leopard rocks.

He stumbles over an obstacle in the path. Bending his head down he looks directly at a bunch of purple bell-shaped flowers, fanning out like a bouquet. He's never seen these flowers on the mountain.

Next to the flowers, blurry in the pale morning light, he sees the obstacle he stumbled over on the ground: an arm reaching above a head, pointing toward the lake in the east. A face is barely recognizable as such: broken bones pierce the bloodied skin. Wisps of blond hair above the forehead are matted by clumps of blood and red mud from the path. Below a blond-bearded chin, on the neck extending out of a filthy army fatigue, a tattoo is etched into the pale skin at the jawline: a swastika. Next to the body, marred by bits of bloody skin, sits the murder weapon: a big, black-onyx speckled leopard rock.

Greg takes a deep breath. *I know what to do. I used to wear a police uniform.* With the tip of his boot, he gently nudges the body. Nothing. Checks the pulse at the neck. There's no life left. He looks like he's been dead for a few hours. Greg will not touch it further. He will go back down to the cabin and report his find to the sheriff's department in Juniper. One of the deputies will come and investigate the death.

Well, that's what would happen under normal circumstances. In the world as it was a month ago, when citizens could expect a certain protection and some form of law enforcement. But they are far from that world.

He protects his family as best as he can and tries to provide for them without expecting outside help. Getting the sheriff involved might endanger rather than help. As they have experienced in town, the Neo-Nazis act with impunity and the sheriff gives them free reign. The dead body appears to be one of them. And they're dangerous. Stevie is still limping and he's lucky his jaw was not broken.

He surveys the crime scene and then makes his way back down Kosmik Peak as the sun breaks free from the mountain. After a moment of beauty, its light turns harsh and unforgiving. He needs to consider the bare facts of the situation before making a hasty decision.

A bludgeoned Neo-Nazi lies on the path of their

mountain. Where there's one, there are usually more. He has to play this right, or the Neo-Nazi will not be the only one bludgeoned.

GREG HURRIES BACK and enters the cabin to find nine people ranging in age from nine to eighty-five sitting around the table—a table designed for six in a cabin built for four. They look up expectantly. *What am I going to tell them?* Vega smiles, but after seeing his face she raises her eyebrows in an unspoken question. She knows something's wrong.

"You were out early." She gets up to offer Greg her seat. He sits down in front of a cup of weak coffee—Hilde brought her hand-cranked coffee grinder, bless her heart —and a bowl of hot cereal cooked with water, not milk. He doesn't want to say anything. Doesn't want them to worry quite yet.

"Everything alright?" asks his older son, Daniel. He's finished his breakfast and is drawing the faces of the people around the breakfast table in his sketchbook.

Eighty-four-year-old Hilde stirs her cereal nervously.

"Can I go outside and play with Midnight?" says Eleni. She sits on the floor with the black Lab and brushes his fur. He seems to enjoy it.

In addition to ten people, there's also Midnight to feed and shelter. He's always underfoot. Greg gave the dog to his mother and sister after Midnight's retirement as search-and-rescue scent dog.

"We have to work on your reading and writing first, Eleni," Tarek says.

Too many people with too many needs.

VEGA:

Something's wrong. Something serious. Vega can see it in the furrow on Greg's brow. Not that anything has been right since the solar storm.

"Vega, I need to talk to you," he says.

"Of course."

"Downstairs."

Really serious. Everybody at the table is quiet. They look at Vega expectantly. She shrugs her shoulders, gets up and slips into a jacket. Inge starts to collect the breakfast bowls for cleaning.

Greg and Vega step into a sharp westerly wind as they open the door to the outside stairs leading to the basement. The bottom floor of the cabin has been built into the mountainside where the temperature is always moderate—not too cold in winter, not too hot in summer. They had planned to turn it into a wine cellar—before the solar flare. Now it stores sacks of oatmeal, rice, dry beans, potatoes, conserved jars of tomatoes, jam and two ten-gallon canisters of olive oil. It's also where Daniel and his girlfriend Lin are sleeping. They have partitioned off one part of the space and set up their bed on palettes down here, where they have their own entrance door, a window to the west, and privacy. Daniel has tacked up his drawings of the trees and animals they can see on the slope. It's not too bad, considering.

Greg sits on an old garden chair next to a box of turnips and beets.

Vega sits down on a big bag of coffee beans. "What's up Greg?"

"I found something on the path to Kosmik Peak."

"What?"

"Actually, I found someone." He twitches uncomfortably.

"We really can't take in another person, especially after Hilde, but we can feed them and send them on their way."

"That won't be necessary," Greg says gruffly. "He's dead."

There it is. "I knew something was really, really wrong when you walked in."

"I'm not sure what to do with him," Greg says.

It's very rare that Greg admits uncertainty. He always knows what to do.

"Get the sheriff." It seems obvious.

"The dead man has a swastika tattoo on his neck, and he was bludgeoned to death with a leopard rock on our mountain. It wasn't an accident or a mountain lion."

"You think the sheriff will blame us?"

Greg nods grimly.

"The longer we wait, the worse it's going to get."

The door opens to a gust of cold air, and Stevie walks in. Even though it's early spring it can still be chilly up here at this altitude.

"Mom, Dad, what's going on?" He confronts them.

"Nothing," Vega looks at her twenty-five-year-old son and wishes she could spare him the details of Greg's discovery.

"Don't lie to me. I left Los Angeles, my career, friends, and the life I built without help from you. But now that I'm back, you treat me little a little boy. Keep me in the loop. I can help."

Greg sighs. "Okay Stevie, sit down."

He tells Stevie about his find. A dozen possibilities run through Vega's mind. None of them pleasant, promising, or safe.

"There's really just one thing to do. We have to get rid of the body," Stevie says.

Greg nods. "Will you help me?"

"Of course."

"Where there's one Neo-Nazi, there will be more. The *Superior Bastards* will be all over us," Vega says.

"That's why we have to get rid of him, Mom."

"They'll come and look for him."

"We'll deal with them when that happens." Greg has made up his mind.

He and Stevie look at each other and nod.

"Don't worry Vega. We'll handle it. Don't tell anybody else."

Vega bites her lower lip, a habit she has when she disagrees, but tries to hold her tongue. She still thinks they should report this to the sheriff, but she'll go along. For now.

She knows sitting around in this crowded house with nothing to do drives Stevie crazy. Daniel has his girlfriend Lin, grandma Inge has her daughter Rose and her friend Hilde, Greg and Vega have each other, and Tarek has his daughter Eleni. But what does Stevie have? Nobody and nothing. He sleeps on a mat in the loft in his parents' bedroom. He just got beat up by a Neo-Nazi. There's no future for him except to sit around and wait until food supplies run out, or until they're attacked by desperate scavengers. He's twenty-five years old and these are his prospects.

STEVIE:

Stevie grabs a rope and some rags from the piles in the basement. He pulls on an old work shirt while Vega heads back upstairs. She'll figure something out to keep the others calm. He and his dad climb silently shoulder to shoulder up the steep hill. His shin still hurts, but it's not broken.

It occurs to Stevie that he needs to start daily defense drills. Target practice, katana training. Stockpile rocks on the deck that can be thrown at attackers. Turn this unwieldy bunch into a disciplined defense force. Stevie stumbles and looks down at one of those strange, black-spotted leopard rocks.

"Right around this corner, by those purple flowers," Greg says.

Stevie hasn't seen a corpse since he was a little kid and found a dead Mexican artist in a canyon in the desert. But the artist had been pretty far away. This body is right in front of him, and the face is a bloody mess. Flies around the eyes, maggots eating away at the wound. Vomit rises in Stevie's throat, but he swallows hard. Not in front of his dad. He looks up at a sugar pine and takes a deep breath of pine-scented air to distract himself, before he looks again. Wisps of blond hair between clots of blood on the head.

"Okay, let's go Stevie," Greg says impatiently. Of course, this does not faze him. He's seen lots of corpses in his former job as a police officer.

"Put on your gloves and grab the legs."

"Where are we taking him?"

"We'll throw him down the mountain."

Stevie pulls his bandana over his mouth and nose against the smell, not because he is afraid of catching anything. Nobody gives a shit anymore. They're way past worrying about getting sick. They have a lot worse to be afraid of. Looking at the flies on the bloody face makes him gag again. Trying to grab the ankles of the dead man, stuck in scruffy combat boots, he feels something soft and squishy and liquid underneath the leather. Repelled, he lets it drop.

"Pull yourself together," Greg says.

"It's broken, I think."

"Nothing we can do about that now."

Stevie bends over to pick up the legs again, while his dad gets hold under the shoulders.

They both hear it at the same moment. Steps on the trail, coming toward them. They freeze. A rock tumbles down the incline. The dead man's compatriots, looking for him? How many? What do they have to defend ourselves? Greg motions to the bushes.

The manzanita and mountain lilac brush is dense along the trail, but too low to hide behind. Greg steps away from the body and off the trail on the downhill side. Branches and underbrush crack loudly. Stevie looks around for a weapon, picks up a sturdy branch. The steps stop.

"Who's there?" Lin's voice, then a bark—Midnight.

"It's just us. No worries." Stevie can hear relief in his father's voice.

Lin walks around the bend with Midnight straining at his leash. He's trying to get to Stevie, and whimpers happily.

"What are you doing here?" Lin stops and stares down at the body.

"What does it look like?" Greg asks, ambling out of the brush. "We're cleaning up."

Stevie looks at Lin. Is she going to freak out?

Lin doesn't ask any questions. He guesses she doesn't need to. She already assessed the situation.

"Okay," Lin says. "Where are we going to take him?"

"Take one of the legs and carry him to the rim." Greg commands.

Lin ties Midnight to a tree and grabs the left leg, the squishy one Stevie just dropped. She doesn't even bat an eye. He takes the other leg and together they carry the body to the edge of the mountain, where the terrain drops down into a steep ravine.

"We'll have to heave it a bit to throw it far enough down. He can't get stuck on top," Greg says.

"Got it," Lin says and Stevie nods. "How long has he been dead?" she asks.

"Not long, maybe a day."

It hadn't occurred to Stevie to ask, but of course it's important to find out when he was killed.

"Ready? Swing to the right."

They swing three times, higher and higher each time, and then let go on Greg's command. The dead man flies high and pretty far. *Please, don't get stuck on top of a tree,* Stevie pleads silently. The body lands on brushes and stays there. Shit. You can see him from above. They all just stand and stare. A subtle movement, a branch breaks here, a crack there, slowly the body crashes through the underbrush and the branches close behind him. Now, they can't see him from up here, but they made a hell of a racket. Branches are still breaking; soil is shifting, sliding down the mountain.

"He's going to be hard to find. And hard to get to. In case someone does find him, it'll look like an accident." Greg seems satisfied with their handiwork.

"If you look closely, you can see one boot sticking out of a Manzanita brush," Lin observes, scanning the ravine.

"You have to look very closely and know what you are looking for."

"His comrades will know what to look for. Did you inspect the crime scene?" she turns to his dad.

"The murder weapon was evidently a mid-size leopard rock. It's on the side of the road, but I'm rolling it into the brush. It still bears traces of blood and tissue. He was hit from behind numerous times on the head until he collapsed. The killer must have wielded the rock with both hands, there is no sign that one side of the head was hit harder than the other. Therefore, we have no indication that the perpetrator was either right or left-handed. The victim must have bent down when he was hit. Otherwise, the killer could not have reached enough momentum to crack the victim's skull."

Stevie observes this exchange. Lin's cool, rational question, and his father's detailed, professional answer. He wants to ask a question too. "Why was he here?"

"I have no idea." Greg shakes his head. "This path is

public. Nobody coming up here can be seen from the cabin. But it's a long way from town. Especially without a car. The victim didn't carry a weapon, so he was not out hunting. There was nothing in his pockets. The only identifying markers are his army fatigues and the swastika tattoo."

"Unless the killer took his weapon."

Greg nods with a grim expression. "Let's go back. We're done here." He brushes off Lin's comment and his gloves.

Stevie continues the conversation in his mind with what has not been said. The killer may come back. He needs to strengthen their defenses. Start defense training. This is not going away quietly.

LEAVING Lin and Stevie behind at the drop site, his dad goes back to the cabin. Stevie unties Midnight and they follow.

"I'm glad Daniel wasn't here to see this." Lin walks next to Stevie, who holds the leash. "He is very sensitive. He has a kind nature. Do you know back in San Diego he fed all the neighborhood stray cats?""

"Better not tell that to my dad. He'd be furious. How did you two meet?" Stevie asks.

"At the Environmental Defense Council at the University of California San Diego. Daniel gave a short presentation about energy consumption, back when people still cared about the environment. He cared about the trees, the air, the sky, and all the creatures living on the planet."

"He's always been that way."

"That's what attracted me to him. I was never a fan of macho men. We sat in the circle, and I wore my green mini skirt. I saw him looking at my legs and getting a little distracted. That made me smile."

Stevie grins. Lin does have nice legs.

"After the meeting, we mingled and nibbled on some snacks. I asked Daniel a question. I knew the answer perfectly well, but he gave a long-winded reply, trying hard not to look at my legs. So, I listened and looked at him with rapt attention. I could tell he liked me."

"Understandably." Stevie could fall for someone like Lin.

"I had just won a scholarship to UCSD. I didn't know a soul in San Diego. I told Daniel my family was still back in Korea. Daniel became my family here." Lin's voice sounds husky, as if she's trying to suppress her emotion.

They pass the spot where Greg found the body. No trace is left. Stevie recognizes the spot because of the bunch of purple flowers.

"We had to get rid of the body. We can't be naïve and think we'll be able to live on this mountain peacefully while the world around us goes to pieces. How long can we survive on our supplies? How long before someone discovers we have shelter, food, electricity, water, and heat? All in short supply out there." Lin sounds like she's trying to convince herself as much as she's trying to convince Stevie.

"The Neo-Nazi had to be dealt with. It had to be done." Stevie points to the bruise on his jaw. "We've seen what they are capable of."

"Concealing the body will buy some time, but it won't prevent future attacks. I saw the swastika on his neck. Unfortunately, I know these guys only too well."

"How?"

Lin stops on the track. "A swastika brings up bad feelings and associations for most people. I consider myself a rational and cool-headed person, but in my case, a swastika is not just a historical reminder of a time of terror and genocide in Germany. I personally had a very bad experience with Neo-Nazis. I try not to think about it too much, but that swastika tattoo brought it all back, as if it had happened yesterday."

"Can you talk about it?"

"It's hard. I haven't even told Daniel. It happened on a Saturday afternoon three years ago in Southeast Los Angeles, at my parents' liquor store at the corner of Adams Avenue and Normandie. It's a busy intersection frequented by thirsty USC students more interested in partying than studying. My parents were working hard to get me into UCLA, and I was working hard to get the grades for admission. On weekends I helped out in the store, so my father and mother could rest. Their store was open seven days a week, from eight in the morning until eleven at night. My parents are immigrants from South Korea. They had no complaints about the long hours, but they did appreciate a two-hour nap on a weekend afternoon.

"I sat behind the plexiglass barrier doing my math homework, while my parents slept in the storage room on two foldout cots. I heard my father's snores all the way in the front.

"It was two in the afternoon, quiet time in South LA, when three skinheads entered the store. I looked up and smiled, good Korean daughter that I am. One of them, shaved head, brown beard, a swastika tattooed on his shoulder, clearly visible under the white muscleman shirt, snarled at me. 'What are you smiling at, little yellow bitch?' My smile froze. I tried to be polite. 'How can I help you?'"

Lin stops. Her body goes ridged. Stevie can tell how hard it is to relive this Saturday afternoon.

"'A bottle of your best whiskey, and pronto. The blue label one,' he demanded. I told him we don't carry Blue Label Johnnie Walker. Not enough demand around here, but we have the Black Label. I turned around to get a bottle. Even though I was only seventeen, a senior in high school, I knew my alcohol. I'd grown up in that store."

"That's why you recognized the brands of champagne in Hilde's trunk right away," Stevie remembers.

Lin nods. "The skinhead looked around to his

companions. One of them had ADOLF tattooed on his bare chest. 'Not enough demand? We demand it! We're not your cheap Chinamen, or welfare scum from around here. We're from the Aryan Nation and only the best is good enough for us!' They all laughed at this. The skinhead even went as far as beating his pale chest. I smiled politely and offered to find out which store around there carries Blue Label Whiskey, which runs over $250 per bottle. 'Look at her educating us about whiskey. Acting so superior. You think you are better than us? We're gonna wipe that smile right off your pretty face. Let's go boys!'"

Stevie gasps and takes hold of Lin's arm.

"With that two of them began to attack the plexi-glass barrier separating them from me. They grabbed the edge of the barrier and try to break it loose from the frame. The third skinhead, ADOLF, began smashing the grocery shelves in the center of the store with a metal baseball bat he had brought."

Lin shakes herself out of the memory.

"I don't want that film to unravel any further. It repeats itself over and over in my mind and in my nightmares. I can't stop or control it. That's the reason why I don't feel any remorse about throwing a dead Neo-Nazi down the mountain."

8

DAY 22: STEVIE

Daniel and Lin aim their bows at the large bull's eye target set up in the shade underneath the deck. Daniel pulls the string of his elegant Hickory wooden recurve bow, like Legolas' bow in the Lord of the Rings. Lin uses a black plastic compound bow. Not as pretty, but effective and easy to use. They both let go at the same moment and with a subtle whap their arrows hit the target. Lin hits a perfect score. Daniel's not bad, about two rings out from the center. She'd be good at anything. Stevie asks her to hand her bow to Tarek. Maybe Tarek and Daniel can form the archery section. But Stevie still doesn't trust Tarek, and he questions his brother's aim.

Stevie wants Lin to try her hand at one of the Japanese katana swords.

We'll see how practice goes today. Then we'll decide who is going to use which weapon—meaning, I'll decide.

He is still wondering how to conduct the katana practice. In ancient Japan, the lethally sharp swords were tested by cutting heads off corpses. Good Katanas could cut through up to nine necks in one stroke. The opportunity to practice on a corpse has unfortunately been eliminated since they heaved the only available corpse over the hillside. He's not sure what else to use. Wood is out of the question; it would dull the blades.

Everybody is here, except his dad. Greg's got his Glock and knows how to use it. He told Stevie that he's all for defense training, but he has to work in the wood shed. "Someone has to replenish our firewood to keep us warm," he said.

His Mom, grandma, Hilde, Rose, and Eleni have been assigned to collect rocks and make piles on the deck as ammunition to hurl at attackers from above. They are scrambling to pick up the heavy rocks in buckets and carry them up hill. Stevie sees Inge and Hilde rest on a rock and wipe sweat from their faces. This is obviously too much for them. Stevie feels a twinge of guilt for making them work so hard.

Stevie suggested pouring boiling oil onto the invaders. But his mom argued that they only have two precious ten-gallon can of olive oil left. It can't be wasted. They need it for cooking and it wouldn't go very far as a weapon. She's got a point. He compromised by substituting oil with boiling water to pour over the railing.

His Mom seems a bit lackluster about the new training. He watches her staring into the distance, with one rock in her hands. But young Eleni is totally gung-ho. She runs up and down with Midnight in tow and piles her rocks up on the deck. It gives her something to do, Stevie thinks. *She'll be helpful when the time comes.*

Stevie knows exactly what to say and what to do. He recognizes each person's strength and weaknesses, and how to integrate them with optimal results into their defense force. Lin is using a katana with Stevie in hand-to-hand combat. She's a natural with the katana. Her agility and concentration are razor-sharp as they thrust and parry in hand-to-hand combat. *I'd trust her with my life*, he thinks.

"Have you done this before?" he asks her.

Lin shakes her head and her long hair flies around her face. Her smooth looks are so deceiving; there is a core of steel underneath. Fighting side by side, the two of them will be unbeatable.

Rose and Eleni are still collecting the rocks used as projectiles for the artillery defense on deck. *We'll have to figure out how to build a crenellated shield around the deck, to provide protection as well as gaps for throwing stones.*

Hilde and Grandma retreat into the house to catch their breath and to have a cold drink of water. Stevie decides they won't withstand the rigors of a siege. He makes a mental note to build them a dugout, well camouflaged by branches, where they can hide safely and also guard provisions in case there is a breach. It may remind them of the bomb shelters they had to hide in as children during the war. That experience may strengthen their resolve.

This is what I was meant to do. I found the purpose of my life. When he was a little boy of seven, he had an obsession with zombies. He even built a website to provide the best defense strategies in the eventuality of a zombie attack. Read all the survival guides and, of course, Max Brooks' World War Z was his bible. The grown-ups smiled indulgently at his obsession, but now the time has come to put that early training into practice.

How amazing that at age seven he already knew his destiny was to prepare for this exact moment. He thought his purpose in life was to write books, maybe make movies, but he was wrong. This is his calling. The lives of ten people depend on him—and his Dad. But Stevie has to organize them, strategize, train, and prepare them.

He smiles at little Eleni who looks at him for approval, her face flushed from running up and down.

"Great job, Eleni," he praises her. She's fast, smart, agile, and confident. She immediately grasped his instructions.

.   .   .

VEGA:

Stevie's training session finally ended. Vega is out of breath and has withdrawn to her flat rocks to cool down. Stevie's enthusiasm rubbed off on the rest of his troops. It's probably good for morale, as long as it's just a game. Something to occupy their time. She's playing along, playing war. He's young. He has a whole life worth fighting for. *I love him for his spirit and his energy.*

But she asks herself how she wants to spend the last months, weeks, or days of her life. Who knows how much time they have? Does she want to fight, rally, practice, or prepare for the transition? Does she want to live in denial, defiance, hope or acceptance?

The branches of the black oak tree cast speckled sunlight on her rock. Tender pink buds at the tips of every branch are bursting into leaves and tassels in the hesitant warmth. Spring is Vega's favorite time of year. A season of hope, anticipation, and reemerging energy after the winter. The valley spreads out below her, bright green meadows sprinkled with a few houses and splashes of trees and underbrush. *This may be our last spring on this mountain. The last time we see the yellow daffodils and red tulips dot the slope. It feels like farewell.*

Will she ever again be able to watch the snow fall in thick, silent flakes while she sits by the fire? Will she make the first footprints in the virgin snow the next morning? Sled down the driveway? Will she see her boys married, meet her grandchildren? Will she see the trees she planted grow tall enough to give shade? She has to let go of all these dreams, and just focus on what they still have. *We're still together.*

Instead of enjoying her 'Golden Years' as Greg puts it, she's back in mother mode, protecting the family at all cost. If she has to lay down her life for them, she'll do it gladly. But sometimes it takes more courage to let go than to fight.

A light breeze stirs the young oak tree and shakes its shadow into a trembling dance. The wind carries an idea. She will start a bi-weekly meditation and mindfulness practice to balance Stevie's defense training. Maybe include some gentle yoga exercises to ease the tension in the body as well as the mind. It will be the perfect supplement to the fighting and the adrenaline that comes with the constant threat of a looming attack after discovering the dead body.

Greg and Stevie got rid of the body. This 'body' was once a man. A mother's son. Someone took care of him until he grew old enough to look after himself. Apparently, he had a swastika tattoo. Vega doesn't know why and when he acquired it, where he lived, and if he was a good man. It's hard to be a good person during these times when everyone just tries to survive. Who took his life? Are they in immediate danger?

A blue jay in the branches of a live oak above her twitters as if in confirmation. "How are you doing today?" she asks him. He cocks his head quizzically. "Better than us humans, I bet." He flashes his iridescent blue wings and alights from the branch in a graceful curve. Watching him float up toward the deck of the cabin and into the sky, she experiences an unexpected moment of joy.

9

DAY 37: GREG

The cool, early morning air feels good on Greg's skin. He is taking Tarek out hunting, but he also wants to feel him out, get to know his motivations, his strengths and weaknesses.

"We are looking for wild turkeys," he tells Tarek. "You can squeeze the turkey caller. It may bring them out."

Tarek operates the device. It makes a guttural, rusty sort of call, similar to a turkey gobble. "How long, do you think we can hold out?" he asks.

"It depends how good we get at hunting." Greg inspects his net and a rope tied into a noose to catch one of the tough old birds. "We want to catch them intact, because shooting shreds the meat, and our ammunition is limited. We're not picky. We'll catch a quail, a grouse, or a pheasant. Like turkeys, they can't fly away, they just flutter a bit."

They have to watch their step on the steep slope, ducking under Manzanita and Ceanothus shrubs.

"So, how did you come to this country? After Aleppo?"

"We were under bombardment from the Russians. A small group of independence fighters were still holding out in the center of town. As an engineer, it was my job to keep the water system working for the civilians. A hopeless task. In April 2013, the Syrian government and their Russian allies had agreed to a ceasefire to evacuate the civilians left in the city. I carried my baby Eleni, wrapped in blankets. It was a sunny morning. In the other hand, I held a suitcase with a few belongings. My wife lagged behind, with another suitcase and bags full of food and baby items. It was going to be a long journey. The buses waited at the meeting place ahead. I allowed myself a moment of hope. Suddenly, a humming filled the air overhead and a sharp whistling sound whipped through the empty street. Then the explosion. The impact threw me onto the ground. I shielded Eleni's tiny body with mine. My ears were ringing. I couldn't hear, couldn't understand what happened. Somebody pulled me up, dragged me to the buses. 'My wife,' I shouted and tried to go back." Tarek stops and stares off into space, toward the distant mountains.

"I'm very sorry." Greg feels uncomfortable for bringing up this painful experience of Tarek losing his wife, Eleni's mom. He decides to stop digging into Tarek's past. He's not good at dealing with other people's grief. Or with his own, for that matter.

They keep walking, making a lot of noise, which probably gives the birds plenty of warning. But the air is fresh, and the scent of the emerging purple mountain lilacs fills the air with anticipation for spring.

Greg stops. Voices come from below. A shot rings out.

"Greg, did you ...?"

"No, hunters," Greg whispers.

Branches crack and crackle ahead. They stand stock-still. Greg distinguishes two voices: "All right, we got another one." The second voice: "Nice shot." A high-pitched whine and the flutter of wings. Turkeys, scrambling to escape. Footsteps coming their way. Greg feels a twist in his gut but stands his ground, weapon drawn. The underbrush before them opens and out stumble—not very gracefully—two men, each holding a dead turkey by its legs.

"Drop the turkeys! Hands above your head!" Greg commands and clicks the safety switch on his Glock.

"Hey," one of the guys, a burly one with a black scraggly beard, shouts and throws his dead turkey at them, while diving for his weapon with the other hand. At lightning speed, Greg shoots at him, barely missing his hand and hips. His mouth is dry, but he fights the rising fear. He must appear strong. The intruders get the message. Both drop their weapons and raise their hands.

"Tarek, take the guns and the turkeys." Greg still points his weapon at the intruders. "Who are you?" he demands, once they've been disarmed and relieved of their bounty.

"Who wants to know?" the burly guy, with a grimy MAGA baseball hat and army fatigue jacket asks.

"I'm asking the questions here. You're on my land." Greg assumes a commanding tone.

"Fuck that, I don't care who owns this land."

"You can't hunt here."

Greg keeps his gun steady, while he motions to Tarek to tie up their hands with rope.

MAGA man laughs. "No hunting, my ass! The rules have changed! Every man for himself. We're claiming this land as ours."

"You're pretty loud for someone at gunpoint with his hands tied. This land is already claimed."

They stare at each other in a sort of stalemate. Greg has the upper hand—at the moment. MAGA man is wearing a black t-shirt with 6MWE printed in yellow. Greg has no idea what that stands for. The man turns toward Tarek with an expression of disgust.

"And who have we here? I respect a white man who defends his land, but you're hanging out with an Arab? Consorting with the enemy, aren't you?" They both laugh.

Greg sees Tarek's face turn red with anger and fear.

"None of your business. He's with me and this is my land. I'm patrolling it. Stay off. Trespass, and I'll shoot you." Outwardly Greg is unfazed, but inwardly he's terrified. He wonders how many more men and riffles are under these Bastards control.

"Look, we don't want any trouble," says the second man, a skinny kid with pimples and dirty jeans that are much too big for him.

"Shut up, Johnny," MAGA man hisses. "Trouble is our middle name."

"I'll let you go, this time. But if you ever come back ..." Greg motions with his gun down the mountain.

"We're not leaving without our guns and our turkeys." MAGA man demands.

"We're keeping 'em."

"You can't do that. We have fifteen men to feed!" Johnny pleads.

"Let 'em keep one of the turkeys," Tarek says. "We're only ten people."

"Shut up."

MAGA man stares at Tarek with glee. "Well, that's good to know."

"Take a turkey and get out. Next time you won't get away that easily."

"What about our guns?"

"Confiscated." Greg searches each guy for additional weapons and finds extra ammunition in MAGA man's pocket.

The Bastard glares at him with hatred.

"Did you see our buddy, Jack? Blond beard, around your size?" Johnny's voice sounds shrill.

"No. Get out now, before I change my mind." Greg waves his gun at Johnny.

"How are we supposed to carry the turkey? He tied our hands," Johnny motions at Tarek with his chin.

"That's your problem."

Tarek takes one of the turkeys and puts the neck into Johnny's tied hand. Grunting, they stumble off toward the dirt road.

Greg and Tarek are alone in the clearing, one wild turkey at their feet.

Tarek plops down on a rock. He wipes the sweat from his brow.

"Sorry about their taunt, Tarek, but we need to show strength. They have fifteen men, and you told them we are only ten. What do you think they're gonna do to us?"

"Oh shit. I messed up."

Greg shakes his head. "I want you to stay at the cabin from now on. I'll take Stevie or Lin with me. We have to increase patrols."

"Because I'm an Arab? And a Muslim?" Tarek challenges. "At least I didn't reveal that six of us are women, two of them very elderly."

Greg shrugs. "No reason to provoke a confrontation. It's for your own good."

"Who were they talking about? Jack? Blond beard?"

"Keep that to yourself, Tarek. I don't want to worry the others."

"He came here, this Jack?"

"Yeah."

"And?"

"Let's just say he's not going back," Greg takes a few big steps back up the hill and Tarek follows, panting to keep up.

"But they will come looking for him," Tarek says between shallow breaths.

10

DAY 38: STEVIE

Stevie is working on the dugout with his Dad, Daniel and Tarek. The location they chose is perfect. It's not too close to the cabin to be seen and not too far to reach quickly in an emergency. Tarek, always the engineer outlined the shape with rope. It's big enough for four people to sleep inside. They are digging three feet deep into the ground.

"It will be warmer that way, and we have more stability and less walls to build," Tarek explains.

"You're sure we won't be visible from the cabin?" Daniel asks.

"No, the trees and underbrush are too dense." Tarek points at the ceanothus brush with his shovel. "Being dug low into the ground will help with camouflage."

"Hey, we can use it to hide from the wrath of Rose," Stevie jokes.

Tarek frowns.

"Hopefully we won't ever need it." Daniel changes the subject. "It'll be pretty cold out here."

"The depth inside the ground adds some insulation." Tarek has already considered the temperature.

"We'll bring blankets and sleeping bags, and look at the Black Market for thermal mats," Greg says.

Stevie wonders what the chances are. Such items are probably worth more than food these days. But it's good to be working outside with the guys. Sometimes there's too much female energy in the cabin.

Stevie told Vega they need her help to allocate provisions for the dugout. Nonperishables that will provide the basics in case they have to retreat to the shelter. If the rest of the group won't make it, then at least the two elder women and Eleni will have enough water and won't starve for a while. But he also wants to talk to her about her meditation classes. Vega scrambles down the path with two bags full of water containers and canned food.

"Put it down here," Greg says and clears a spot on the ground.

"Looks good, guys," Vega sits down on one of the camping chairs. "How are you going to make the roof?"

"Imagine an airport hangar, with a rounded, semi-cylindrical roof span. We'll bend branches across the top, then weave in other branches like a basket, perpendicularly for camouflage, and line it on the inside with a transparent tarp I found in the garage." Tarek has it all thought through. He turns out to be quite an asset.

Stevie is leaning on his pick ax enjoying the short break from digging and feeling the warm sun on his back, waiting for the right moment to confront Vega.

"Nice. And the floor?"

"We'll elevate it with those wooden boards left over from the house construction. Then we cover it with canvas drop cloth and a few old rugs," Tarek turns back to work on the structure.

This is Stevie's opportunity to corner his mother out of earshot from the others. He leans over her in a confrontational posture. He needs to get her attention. "Mom, what the hell do you think you are doing?"

"Calm down, Stevie," Greg says and pulls him back at the shoulders.

Vega's eyebrows shoot up in her face, bewildered. "What did I do?"

"You're telling everybody that through meditation they can learn to accept things as they are, whether agreeable or disagreeable."

"What's wrong with that? It's actually a quote by Suzuki Roshi."

"You're telling them to give up and accept whatever is happening? That's crazy!"

"Stevie, don't get all worked up." Greg puts his hand on Stevie's arm.

"But it just confuses them!" Stevie insists.

"It decreases people's anxiety. They're scared and stressed." Vega says calmly, which makes him even more furious.

"It's the wrong attitude. They'll be in no shape to fight. Do you want us all to die?"

Vega looks at Stevie with a sweet smile, and even reaches out her hand to touch him, but he recoils.

"Stevie, I'm ready to defend you, and I'm willing to die for you. But I also want to be prepared for the transition to the next stage of existence—when it comes."

He turns to his father in frustration. "Dad, please talk some sense into her."

"Vega, we are in a precarious situation. We have to work together, not against each other," Greg says reasonably.

"I absolutely agree." She nods vigorously.

"But you're undermining everything I'm trying to do, Mom. You can't think that way, or else they'll just surrender. The Bastards are looking for their missing member, Jack. They won't give up."

"That's why we need to find out who killed him," Vega says reasonably.

"We need to stay calm and rational. We want to avoid a confrontation," Greg cautions.

"How is finding the murderer going to help?" Stevie asks.

"We can tell them who it is, and they will leave us alone."

All three of them are silent for a moment.

"And how are you suggesting we do that?" Stevie doesn't like the expression on his mother's face. She looks like she knows more than she admits.

"We have to find out why the victim was here and who had a motive to do him harm."

"How are we going to find out, Vega? We can only speculate that he came here to check out the layout for a hostile take-over. I saw these Superior Bastards at the Black Market and when I went hunting with Tarek. They beat up Stevie. They're not messing around. They have weapons and will use them." Greg says reasonably.

"If that's why he was here, then who had the most reason to take him out?" Vega still looks completely calm, which infuriates Stevie.

"Mom, what are you implying? Are you saying the killer was one of—"

"Whoever it was, his Neo-Nazi buddies are looking for him. They know he was here. We need to assert ourselves here on this mountain. A show of power may be necessary."

She can't disagree with Greg's excellent point.

"I'm just suggesting to look at this from their point of view. They're also just trying to survive. They had no warning this disaster was coming," she says.

Stevie can't believe what she just said. "Mom, have you

ever even seen these Neo-Nazis? You know what they're going to do to you when they come here looking for their dead comrade on the mountain?"

"I saw a program about them on Frontline."

He shakes his head. "Do you even realize how ridiculous you sound? They have fifteen armed men. Tarek told them we are only ten. They suspect us of killing Jack. And one of them wore a 6MWE T-shirt."

"What does that mean?" Vega asks, demonstrating how little she really knows about Neo-Nazis.

"Six Million Wasn't Enough," Dad explains.

"Six million what?"

"Jews!" Stevie yells at her and she cringes.

"Okay, both of you, time out. We need to find a compromise here." Greg is physically pushing them apart. "You can continue your yoga classes, but don't undermine Stevie's defense strategy, and don't talk to them about 'surrender' and 'unconditional acceptance.' That's not going to help. Maybe you can stress fitness, and preparedness, and presence of mind? That would be helpful."

"Okay, no problem. But preparedness for what?"

Stevie sighs. She always has to have the last word.

11

DAY 40: VEGA

Vega is sitting at the living room table, looking through cookbooks trying to find a recipe to cook a wild turkey. It has to be marinated at least three days in buttermilk to soften the tough flesh. She doesn't have buttermilk, but she can make a salty brine with herbs. At the other end of the table, Rose and Eleni are practicing math. From the view nook, where Inge and Hilde sleep, she hears their conversation.

"I'm still grateful I made it safely up here. Driving alone up this mountain in the dark was crazy. Thanks to Stevie's call, I knew where to go," Hilde says. "I love to watch the sun reflecting golden off the ocean in the afternoon, and layers of hills and valleys in between. After sunset, I can watch Venus and the moonrise in the glorious night sky, divided by the Milky Way. I never saw stars at home. The city lights were too bright. I couldn't see the ocean either, even though I lived much closer to it."

"The view is very nice from here," Inge agrees. "I like the wildlife. Look at the blue jay on the railing of the deck outside the window. How its blue feathers reflect the light!"

"I feel safe here. And you, Inge, are my best friend. We lived through WWII as young girls. We both lost our fathers early, casualties of the Wehrmacht. We survived the post-war period in our bombed-out cities, with barely any food or fuel. Compared to those years, this current situation is a piece of cake. We have food, firewood, a place to sleep and we have each other."

"Yes, for now we do," Inge says cautiously.

"Let's not go down that path. I'm very good at living in the moment. Making the best of it. *The moment is all we have*, as my late husband, Jerome, used to say. And the moment, right now, is good—even though my stash of champagne and caviar is gone," Hilde laughs. "At home, I sat alone in a big empty house. I had lots of space and a big bed, but I couldn't see the path of the sun in the sky. Now I share the dinner table with nine friends."

"As long as the food will last," Inge's voice sounds skeptical.

"Come on, Inge. We should go and see this hideout place they are building for us. Vega already brought down some provisions."

"Sure, I wouldn't mind a bit of fresh air." Inge audibly gets up from the sofa.

"They should let Vega guard the supplies in the hideout. She doesn't seem to like the defense training. I enjoy Stevie's practice sessions, even though I get a bit out of breath."

"So, you don't like Vega's meditation and yoga classes?" Inge asks.

"Not really. I don't want to be ungrateful, but just sitting around, trying to calm down doesn't work for me."

Vega has noticed Hilde's restlessness at the meditation sessions. After two weeks, she stopped coming.

Inge smiles. "She wants to ease the tensions."

"She makes me feel even more antsy."

Rose pushes the room divider aside noisily. "Can you chat somewhere else? We're trying to concentrate here."

"Sorry, we'll get out of your way."

"Some people still have work to do and can't afford to sit around and get fed and pampered." Rose looks straight at Hilde and pushes her hair out of her face with an impatient gesture.

Vega sees Hilde's face burn red with shame and embarrassment.

"Rose, that wasn't necessary. Don't make her feel bad," Inge chides her daughter.

"She's not even family."

Vega is just about to intervene, but Inge seems to handle it just fine.

"To us she is." Two bright red dots appear on Inge's cheeks. "Let's go check out our hide-out, Hilde."

Rose stomps out, while Hilde puts on her sturdy shoes.

"Don't listen to her," Inge says. "She doesn't mean it."

"She does mean it. I'm an extra mouth to feed."

When they walk into the main room, Vega and Eleni sit at the table, both engrossed in books.

The two elders grab their walking sticks and carefully make their way down the steep slope dotted with yellow daffodils.

"Aren't they beautiful?" Hilde voice drifts in through the open glass door to the deck.

"They are, but they are also quite poisonous. That's why the deer don't eat them. They know better."

Loud voices and the sound of hammering lead them in the direction of the hideout.

Hilde calls out a warning, "You guys better keep your voices down, or else this hide-out won't stay hidden long."

The voices fall silent.

LIN:

Lin sits on a log with Daniel. A faint sound drifts up from below.

"Shh, quiet. I hear something." Lin tries to pinpoint the direction the laughter is coming from.

The wind whispers in the brush oak, and a crow caws overhead. Faint laughter drifts over the hillside.

"Who's laughing?" Daniel asks.

"I'll find out. You stay here." Lin gets up and moves downhill.

"Lin, it's too dangerous. Don't go."

"It's only laughter. What can be so dangerous about that?" Lin slips off down the hillside. The laughter gets louder. Someone's gasping for air. She climbs down the hidden trail next to the black oak to the flat rocks.

Lin hasn't been to the hideout they're building for Hilde and Inge yet, but it must be close by; the source of the laughter. She sees a large hole in the ground. A few leafy branches form a makeshift roof. In the shade underneath, Inge and Hilde sit on camping chairs, holding red plastic cups, a half-empty bottle of whiskey between them.

"And then I ran after the truck and picked up the potatoes as they were tumbling out. I carried them home in my apron. Boy, did we have a feast that night. They tasted even better knowing I stole them." Inge lifts her plastic cup in salute and takes a big swig.

"When the Nazis retreated, the Russians moved in. One Russian soldier came to our door, looking for Nazis and anything in a skirt. Of course, only women and girls were left. As he came in, my mother stood behind the door and hit him over the head with a frying pan. He collapsed right away." Hilde remembers. They erupt in bursts of laughter. "I was so proud of her."

"Shh, we can hear you all over the mountain," Lin warns them. They're so sloshed they haven't even noticed her yet.

"Oops," Hilde giggles.

"Ach du Lieber," Inge tries to compose herself.

Lin shakes her head. "At least you're having a good time, swapping war stories."

They nod, giggling. Lin picks up the bottle and looks at the label.

"You found Greg's stash of single malt Scotch." Lin recognizes the label. She still knows her alcohol.

More suppressed giggles. "Have one." Hilde pours and hands her a red plastic cup, generously filled.

Lin accepts with a shrug. What does she have to lose? The alcohol burns in her throat, and she feels it running down hot into her stomach. A wave of relaxation spreads through her body, and she realizes how tense she's been. She hasn't slept well in weeks. The nightmares are back. Maybe she should take a nap in the hammock this afternoon.

LIN CLIMBS into the hammock under the deck and rocks gently back and forth. Tarek sits at the picnic bench next to her, reading. She hears the wind rustling, and the squeaking rope of the hammock. She's nodding off to the gentle sound of the wind chime. It's Saturday afternoon ten years ago. She is in there parents' liquor store. Lin's moaning now. The hammock starts to sway wildly, as she's thrashing about.

Someone comes to steady it, so she doesn't fall out. Lin screams. "Get away from me!" She wakes up and finds Tarek stroking her face, which glistens with sweat.

"Lin, it's me, it's okay, you're safe …"

She opens her eyes. "Tarek, what are you doing here?"

"You had a nightmare. You almost fell out."

She holds on to his hand. "Thank you for holding the hammock."

"What were you dreaming?" he asks gently.

"I dreamt about the Saturday afternoon that changed my life." She stares into the distance, and he holds on to her hand.

"Can you talk about it?"

Lin shakes her head, but then she begins. "I was a teenager in my parents' liquor store in South LA. Two skinhead Neo-Nazis wedged a switchblade into the plexi-glass borders separating me from them. I backed off toward the racks of alcohol. I knew it was time to wake my parents who were napping in the back room. I yelled at them to call the police. They scrambled to my side, hair tousled, and clothes wrinkled from sleep. 'Run, daughter. Go out the back way. We'll handle this," my father called to me. 'Be a good daughter. Do us proud.' I didn't want to leave them.

The plexiglass started to show cracks. 'Get help, call the police,' my mother pleaded, as she prepared to defend herself with a metal pole. I took one last look at the attackers, wild-eyed and crazed, yelling 'Let's clean this neighborhood of the Asian cockroaches.' I hugged my mom and her pole, as best as I could and told her that I loved her. Then I ran out the back. It was the last time I saw my parents alive."

Tears run down Lin's cheeks and Tarek hugs her awkwardly. He is crying too.

Lin looks at his face and sees his pain. "What about you? What happened to you?"

"It was April 2013 at the evacuation of Aleppo. The Russians broke the cease fire." Tarek shakes with silent sobs. Lin squeezes his hand harder. "The Red Crescent volunteer pushed me into the bus, where I fell into a seat, Eleni still in my arms, crying. 'I'm sorry, your wife's gone.' The volunteer put his hand on my arm. 'We have to get out, or there'll be more casualties.' So, our long journey began, through Turkey, Greece, Bulgaria, Rumania, Hungary, Austria, Germany. At every stop there were signs: 'No migrants! Go Home!' Nobody wanted us, every door shut in our face, until Germany."

A scrap of a sentence from upstairs floats down and pulls him out of his memory. He tries to pull away, tries to pull himself together.

"You're okay now. It's over. We're both fine." Lin is stroking his hand.

"Really? You think this is a place where the color of my skin and my religion is of no importance? Greg put me under house arrest because he thinks my presence as a Muslim will incite these Neo-Nazis. Maybe he's right, but it makes me feel like an outcast and a liability."

Lin's heart goes out to him. She can understand his pain and helplessness as a father of a young girl confronted with such hatred.

"What's going on here?" Daniel has rounded the corner of the house and is standing right in front of the hammock. Tarek quickly lets go of Lin.

"Lin had a nightmare," he explains, "about how she lost her parents."

Lin's face turns into an ugly grimace.

"She didn't lose her parents, they're back in Korea." Daniel protests.

Tarek shakes his head in confusion, looking at Lin.

Lin erupts in sobs.

"What did you do to her?" Daniel asks with a raised voice.

"Nothing, I tried to console her ..."

"Get away from her! Get away from us! We don't want you here, /you don't belong!"

Tarek turns around and runs, down the hill—to where, he doesn't know.

"Why did you tell him your parents are dead?" Daniel asks.

"Because they are."

Lin looks at Daniel with a tear-streaked face. She knows he's not used to seeing her like this. She's always composed, her skin immaculate and smooth.

"You told me they were still in Korea," he says accusingly.

"I couldn't tell you what really happened. It's too painful to think about."

"But you told Tarek?"

"I had a nightmare."

"You've had nightmares before. I was there many times when you woke up at night. Why tell him, and not me?"

She's crying silently, tears rolling down her cheekbones.

"Why couldn't you tell me?" Daniel pleads.

"Because he understands ..."

"Understands what?"

Lin shakes her head. "I felt humiliated, and embarrassed, ashamed. I ran away, while my parents were beaten to death."

"Oh, Lin," Daniel pulls her to him.

Her tight, strong body shakes uncontrollably. "I didn't want you to see me like this. I wanted to be strong. For you."

"You are strong. Much stronger than me. It takes strength to admit a weakness. Let me be here for you. Tell me the whole story. Maybe the nightmares will stop."

Her body feels like a tightly wound spring in his arms. She can't summon her sweet smile to deceive him. He knows she is more powerful than she looks, but he really knows very little about her. Nothing about her regrets and her shame. Only what she chose to tell him, and admittedly, he didn't make a big effort to find out more. He was content to talk about himself, happy that she was interested. He was easily satisfied.

"You assumed I was another smart, hard-driven Asian girl with great potential, and a supportive family, who had sacrificed much to get their daughter into a good American university. Why did you never ask more about my parents?" Lin asks.

"I don't know. Why did you so easily confide to Tarek?" Daniel looks hurt. "You and Tarek seemed to relate to each other quite naturally. What does he understand that I don't?"

12

DAY 41: VEGA

The sky has turned a dirty shade of gray, interrupted by jagged slices of burnt sienna from the setting sun behind a scattered cloud cover.

"Dinner is ready," Vega calls down from the deck to Daniel and Lin below, as if the children were still small and she had to call them in from playing in the garden.

The turkey dinner was supposed to be a celebratory affair, the result of Tarek and Greg's hunting expedition. Greg was a bit vague on the details of how they caught it. After plucking the turkey's feathers, Vega found a bullet of an unfamiliar caliber inside. Not from Greg's Glock. She took it out without mentioning it to anybody. She'll ask Greg for an explanation later, when they are alone.

Vega brined the turkey in salt water for three days to

soften the tough flesh. Then she roasted it in the oven with rosemary and the sweet potatoes Eleni collected from their potato patch. Vega cooked homegrown cabbage and carrots on the side.

Now the entire family is sitting around the table for their mini-Thanksgiving dinner at Easter.

Vega lifts her glass for a toast. "It's not Thanksgiving, but who knows what's going to happen by then, so let's celebrate now ..." She notices an empty chair. Scans the room for who's missing. "Where's Tarek?" she asks.

"I couldn't find him, so I asked Greg to look for him." Rose sits next to the empty chair with Eleni on her other side. "Did you?" she looks at Greg sharply.

"He probably just went for a walk." Vega tries to diffuse her worry.

"In the dark? It's dangerous out there. Why would he do that?" Rose asks with her voice spiraling into higher octaves.

"I took Midnight to look for him. But it's already too dark. We'll have to wait til morning," Greg explains.

"Did you check the hideout?" Stevie asks.

Greg nods. "Nothing's missing."

"So, he didn't plan to stay away," Stevie concludes.

Lin and Daniel exchange worried looks. Something happened. They won't tell, but it's obvious. Rose looks confused. Why would her boyfriend leave?

The black Lab is sitting under the table next to Eleni's chair with his head on her feet. He hasn't left her side.

Vega takes a sip of red wine supplied by Greg's well-stocked wine cellar. She needs a drink. "I'm sure he'll turn up soon," she says, not really believing it herself.

"When is Daddy coming back?" Eleni asks.

"We'll find him, sweetheart," Rose says and strokes her hair.

Eleni starts to cry, and then Rose starts to cry as well.

Stevie and Greg look at each other with grim expressions. Only Hilde and Inge tuck into the platter with potatoes and turkey pieces. They lift their glasses. Vega notices their red cheeks and slightly glassy eyes. Hopefully they are not coming down with something.

"What are you two grinning about?" Rose is raising her voice. "My boyfriend is missing, and you are drinking and laughing. Have you no respect?"

"That's enough, Rose," Inge tells her daughter.

The table falls silent. Even Stevie freezes holding his wineglass midair.

"Let's eat before it gets cold," Vega admonishes.

"Why did he go away?" Eleni wants to know.

"Ask Daniel," Lin says quietly.

Daniel's face turns red. "What's that supposed to mean?" He gets up, looks around the table, challenging. "Now it's my fault that he ran away?"

"Is it?" Eleni asks with a pleading look of her brown eyes.

"We took him in, we protect him and share our resources with him, and then he—"

"Calm down, Daniel," Greg intervenes. "This is enough. Let's eat. No point wasting a good meal for this nonsense." He takes a bite, and a sip of wine.

Daniel sits down reluctantly. He's not looking at Lin. There's trouble in paradise. What happened between these two? Vega wonders.

Dinner passes in strained silence, except for Hilde and Inge, who eat with relish. Most of their life is behind them. They survived a world war. Everything happening now is a bonus. They accept the situation and live in the moment.

Vega looks at Stevie, who chews his turkey meat with determination and a grim set jaw. He looks like he's taking in nourishment to strengthen his body, as if it was another chore. He senses her looking at him, and returns her gaze with anger and defiance in his eyes. *My baby, what happened to you?* She wants to hold him, stroke his back, like she did when he was little.

"I know Tarek didn't leave voluntarily. You know something you're not telling me. This is such bullshit!" Rose erupts.

Vega thinks about the unidentified bullet in the turkey. "Someone wants to tell us where exactly this turkey comes from?" she asks and looks at Greg directly.

"Tarek went hunting with Greg. Greg, you need to let us know what happened. I'm sure it's the reason for his disappearance." Rose insists.

Greg looks very uncomfortable, twitching in his chair.

Vega feels bad for him, but they can't afford to have secrets from each other. Not in their vulnerable situation.

"Okay," Greg relents. "Tarek and I had an encounter on our hunting outing. We met two poachers. They actually shot this turkey."

At least he's fessing up to it, Vega thinks.

Gasps around the table. Especially from Rose and Inge.

"They were hunting on our land, they were trespassing, they threatened Tarek. We drove them away, but ..." Greg pauses.

Rose's voice rises above the others, "Why didn't you tell us? You lied to us!"

"I didn't want to worry you. I did what I thought was the right thing." Greg's voice sounds tired, resigned, weak and full of doubt. Not like a leader.

"This is not protecting us! We need to know. Probably these poachers took Tarek." Rose stands up from her chair and points her finger at Greg.

"Rose, calm down. No point accusing each other," Vega says.

But Rose cannot be stopped. "And I want to know what Daniel did to drive Tarek straight into the arms of these trespassers. Enough of the secrets. They'll get us all killed."

"Let's not exaggerate, Rose," Inge says soothingly.

"What do you have to say, Daniel?" Rose provokes him.

"This is a private matter between Lin, Tarek, and me. Tarek insulted Lin and I got a bit angry, understandably."

Lin makes a face. "It was nothing."

"Enough to drive Tarek away! What did you do to him? It's not a private matter if our safety is at stake!" Rose shouts.

"Our safety has been at stake since the solar storm hit," Vega says quietly.

"And since we retreated to this mountain," Lin adds.

Stevie clears his throat. "Talking about safety. Tomorrow at 8:30 is our next training session. Now more than ever, we need to be prepared. We have a lot of work to do, and not much time," he announces.

People around the table are murmuring, mumbling. Only Lin nods her head and smiles at Stevie.

"Stevie, let us finish our meal," Vega admonishes. This is the nicest meal they have had in many days, and nobody is enjoying it. At least they shouldn't let the food go to waste.

"Mom, will you stop undermining me?"

"Okay, everybody calm down!" Greg has finished his dinner and stretches his long legs under the table.

"We'll clean up," Hilda volunteers, and Inge nods vigorously.

"I'll help." As Eleni speaks Midnight lifts his head and wags his tail.

"Try not to break any dishes," Rose says.

Vega doesn't want to hear Rose's sarcasm and slips out the door to her flat rock for meditation and alone time.

HER MIND IS at two places at once. One part carefully picks its way between the rocks down the steep slope. The other part travels back to a time when Stevie was a six-year-old boy. His flaxen hair reflected the sun like spun gold. When he ran around the garden, orange monarch butterflies landed on his head, drawn by the shiny color and his happy disposition. He would stand still as if in a freeze frame, allow the butterflies to rest, and allow Vega to take a picture of the magical moment.

Afterwards, he'd crawl into his secret garden, over-grown with brambles, to chase after roly-poly bugs that contracted into tight armored balls at the slightest touch. Stevie gently rolled them around on the dirt, delighted with their natural defense mechanism. He'd emerge from the brambles covered in leaves and red berries from the Mexican Peppertree and move on to play with his imaginary friends.

Stevie spent his childhood fluttering from one wonder to the next delight like those butterflies that descended so frequently on his head. Vega misses that Stevie, who was full of stories and happy to share them freely. She doesn't know where that boy went. He must still be somewhere in the serious young man sitting at the table and training the family. Vega mourns that the solar storm has driven that playful Stevie into hiding. It hurts to think that he hates her now and blames her for the way she's dealing with the situation.

Maybe he's right. Like all parents they haven't kept the promise they gave their children when they were small: that this is a safe world full of wonder and pure joy. Like all mothers, she's only human, but because Stevie's childhood was so enchanted, the lessons of growing up were especially painful for him.

Sitting on the rock she stares into the dark sky. A hole in the clouds allows the full moon to spill its mild light onto the hillside. It illuminates a stand of sugar pines trembling slightly in the night breeze. They cast elongated mood shadows down the hill. Despite everything, there is still beauty and wonder in the world.

SHE CLIMBS BACK up the hill in the dark. Under the deck she sees the black silhouette of a figure sitting at the picnic table. She can only see the dark outline. Instinctively she freezes. Who's sitting there in the darkness? White eyeballs reflect the moonlight.

"It's me, Mom." It's Stevie's voice.

"Oh good. I was thinking about you, when you were a boy."

"That's what I want to talk to you about. I'm not a child anymore. I'm a man."

"I know." She sits down next to him in the darkness.

"You're naïve. You live in some kind of a fantasy world, thinking that all is beauty and wonder."

"No, I realize it's not like that, but there still is beauty in the world. Just look up, at Venus setting in the west in the velvety indigo sky."

"Mom, no need to get all poetic on me. I see the evening star. I know the constellations. I can recognize Orion's belt, and the Big Dipper, and the W of Cassiopeia."

"I taught you." She gently puts her hand on his arm, expecting him to shake her off. But he doesn't. At least that's something.

"It's irrelevant."

She sighs. "Let's not argue. Let's just sit here for a while. Watch the night sky."

"You have to stop."

"Stop what?"

"Stop undermining my authority."

"I'm not undermining you, but I won't stop seeing the world as full of wonder."

"But you're wrong. Your way of looking is false; it's a delusion. We just hoisted a dead Neo-Nazi over the cliff. Have you forgotten? And you're encouraging the others in believing in your lies and illusions." Stevie's getting agitated twitching on his seat.

"You used to see the world in a magical light. And the kids around you started to see it your way too."

"I was wrong."

"The world is what we make it to be. We can see it as ugly, or beautiful, but nature just is. It doesn't have a label."

"Stop the philosophizing. I can't take it."

"We used to talk about these questions for hours. Don't you remember?"

"I grew up."

"Thanks to you, I didn't."

He snorts. He's learned how to harden himself. Vega's heart aches for him. It must be so heavy to carry this armor around, just like those little roly-poly bugs he used to play with.

"What about Tarek?" he asks.

"I hope he's going to be okay out there."

"What if the Superior Bastards kidnapped him?" Stevie asks.

"I don't know, Stevie. Tarek has a lot to deal with. He's a Syrian refugee and a single father. I don't think he would abandon Eleni willingly."

"But why did he run away? It's dangerous out there."

"I think he was provoked by Daniel, and some things are more important than our physical safety."

"There we go again, Mom. You're just incorrigible. I'm going to bed."

"Good night, Stevie. I love you."

13

DAY 42: GREG

At first light Greg and Stevie go out with Midnight to find Tarek. The dog is trained in sniffing out the trails of scent. Greg adopted him years ago from the search-and-rescue department, when he turned out to be too friendly for a police dog.

They start at Kosmik Peak for an overview. The peak of their modest mountain has a wooden viewing platform. From here they have a 300-degree view. In the west they can see the rocky El Cajon Mountain whose shape looks like the back of a camel. To the north stretches the low green range of the Palomar Mountains, backed by the San Jacinto Mountains, still spotted with snow in the far distance. In the south, much closer to home is Middle Peak, dotted with the bare trunks of burnt pine trees from the Cedar fire that burned so much wild lands in 2003.

They stare out at the vast space. This space is their refuge, their protection, but it is also a challenge if you try to find somebody. Clouds are piled up in the sky, as if someone had thrown them together in a rush. They move quickly, changing shapes and color, from white to gray.

After sniffing Tarek's favorite red sweatshirt, Midnight is pulling on the leash into the forest. Rushing through the underbrush, they come to a small clearing with a stand of brilliant purple flowers. But then Midnight pulls back toward the road.

It's been light for an hour, but the sun hasn't cleared the mountain range in the east yet. The morning mist still hangs between the fingers of the valley, like white cotton. The air is brisk and cold. It will get warm soon, but wherever Tarek spent the night, he had to find protection from the cold night temperature.

Greg hikes next to Stevie in sullen silence. Something happened between Daniel and Tarek, and now there's tension between Daniel and his brother Stevie. It seems to have something to do with Lin. Greg doesn't want to know, doesn't want to get drawn into the drama. Let them work it out themselves. Vega and Stevie are also at each other. He doesn't want to get involved. Too many people in a small space; obviously there are tensions. That's why he'd rather be out here. Trees don't get their feelings hurt. Rocks don't get anxious about a bruised ego. Birds don't complain. As a matter of fact, they seem to be feeling just fine this morning, judging from their cheerful twitter.

They reach the paved road at the entrance to the dirt path leading to the cabin. Midnight stands in the middle of the road, sniffing the air. He seems confused. Stevie looks at Greg with raised eyebrows.

"The trail ends here. Tarek got into a vehicle. Either by choice or against his will."

"How many people even have cars nowadays?" Stevie asks.

STEVIE:

Stevie and Greg drive the Mustang into Juniper to file a missing person report for Tarek at the sheriff's station. Greg has to navigate around the burnt-out abandoned cars in the middle of the road.

Before they left, Rose was in complete hysterics about her missing boyfriend, or *fiancé* as she calls him now. Eleni didn't want to get up at all and is now lying on the floor with Midnight like a wounded lamb. It's good to get away from the family drama for a bit, but they have to find Tarek; need to bring him back.

The town looks even worse than when he last saw it last. There's trash everywhere. Some still in bags, at the side of the road, others blown into the street by the wind and pecked open by crows, the top scavengers. They seem to thrive in this disaster. There are always some scavengers who feed off trouble— either the human or animal kind.

Greg parks their Mustang in front of the log cabin-style sheriff station at the edge of town, next to a 1950s black-and-white police cruiser with rounded fenders and a red lipstick-shaped emergency light in the middle of the roof. It wouldn't look out of place in an antique car museum!

"Looks like the sheriff's in," Greg says and locks the car door.

The sheriff's station is located in the historical district of Juniper and could be straight out of an old Western, with its wooden portico and old-fashioned sign with lettering on green background. It matches the era of the police cruiser.

Stevie and Greg enter the squeaking swing door and immediately stand in front of Sheriff Baker's massive desk. He's wearing his cowboy hat and drinks a steaming cup of coffee. *Where does he get his coffee?* The sheriff looks up reluctantly.

"What can I do for you, folks?" he asks, as if this was just a normal day during a normal time, which is kind of reassuring.

"We're here to file a missing person report for Tarek Aziz. Here's a picture of him."

The sheriff looks at it thoughtfully. "You up at Kosmik Peak, over by Shelter Valley?" he asks.

Greg confirms this was Tarek's last known location.

"Funny, because I had a missing person report filed just a few of days ago by a local organization." He shuffles through papers on his desk. "A certain Jack Smith was reported missing." He shows them a picture of the man with the blond beard, his swastika tattoo visible above his collar. "Have you seen him?"

Stevie feels a wave of panic rising in his chest.

Greg shakes his head, regretfully. "Was he one of the Superior Bastards?" he says.

"Now, why would you say that?" the sheriff asks sharply.

"Tattoo on the neck."

The sheriff massages his bushy gray mustache. "We can post flyers with your Tarek Aziz's description, but as you may know, I'm policing two hundred square miles from your neck of the woods all the way to Santa Ysabel," he says, making it clear that he won't put much effort into this search. "Maybe I'll come up to your place and look around." It sounds like a threat.

"Where are they located, the Superior Bastards?" Greg asks.

"They took over the old theater off Main Street," the sheriff says, with a cruel grin.

"We might just pay them a visit." Greg maintains a poker face.

No, let's not do that, Stevie thinks. Surprisingly, the sheriff seems to agree with him.

"Now, why would you wanna do that?" the sheriff drawls.

"They've been prowling around our mountain, hunting. Maybe they have our man Tarek."

"Funny you'd be saying that. They think the same about you, that you have their Jack."

"You're welcome to come over to our place and search. We'd appreciate your company when we visit the Bastards. They made some threatening remarks toward Tarek," Greg says.

The sheriff tips back his white cowboy hat and looks thoughtful.

"Tell you what, I'll go over there myself and then I'll come by your place and let you know what I found out. I don't think they'd appreciate your visit."

"Fair enough, sheriff. What about the flyers?"

"We'll post them. But don't hold your breath."

"We won't. See you at our place."

After a short nod, Greg and Stevie exit the station and walk to their car.

"That wasn't very productive," Stevie says once they're back on the dusty road.

"I wouldn't say that. We warned him that the Bastards are hunting and trespassing on our land. We know where they're holed up. We've set things into motion. Now we just have to wait, and hope that Tarek is still alive."

"You're sure they have him?"

"No, but we can drive by the Old Theater and see if they have a vehicle. That would narrow it down. We won't get out of the car." Greg's jaw is set tight.

The Old Theatre is only three blocks from Juniper's center. It's hard to be inconspicuous if you are the only car on the road. Fortunately, the street in front of the Old Theater is littered with abandoned cars, which function as some sort of cover. The Mustang's engine is loud and spews exhaust fumes, but luck is on their side. A group of Bastards is working in a barn at the side of the theater to repair a back-up generator. Their loud voices and focus on the machine, help Greg and Stevie to remain undetected. Sure enough, a historic army transport vehicle with dessert camouflage sits at the curb.

"That's a 1966 M656 8x8 military cargo truck," Stevie says.

Greg turns his head and looks at him surprised. "How do you know that?"

"Call of Duty."

"The video game?" Greg asks, impressed. "They seem to have enough mechanics to keep it running. And gasoline can still be syphoned off easily."

"Now we know they have transportation. They must have taken Tarek."

"He's probably in there." Greg turns to Stevie. "That's all we can do here for today. Let's go to the Black Market. I brought five wine bottles to barter with, and—" he points to the back seat, "A five-gallon water bottle."

"Nice. You didn't bring the Chianti, I hope," Stevie says.

Greg laughs. "No, I know the Chianti is your favorite."

· · ·

VEGA:

Greg and Stevie drove off to Juniper in the red Mustang. They leave gray dust devils in their wake.

Today Vega doesn't want to sit on her flat rock. Today she doesn't want a big view. Today she wants to be inside the forest, covered and hidden by leafy branches. Today she's sitting on a fallen log under a shrub oak tree in the shade. The forest around her is a living, breathing being, and she's just a small part of it. The forest calms her questions about the purpose of life, about the meaning of death, the origin of creation.

Crackling footsteps stir her out of her thoughts. Someone is coming. Who's prowling on their mountain? Someone has found her. Are they the same people who found Tarek? Panic begins to swell in her chest, but she caps it off before it overwhelms her. She takes five deep belly breaths and clears her mind of thought. This is what she has been teaching the very small group who still attend her yoga and meditation classes—Inge, Eleni, Daniel, and Lin. She focusses on being completely in the present moment. The fear subsides. The sounds of the forest return; the wind in the trees, a bird call from across the valley.

And subdued footsteps. Branches are bent, not broken, while small feet gently prod the soft ground. A deer? Midnight appears on his padded paws, followed by

Eleni holding his leash. The two of them have been inseparable.

"You found me." Vega smiles at Eleni and pats the log beside her.

Eleni sits down, looking sad, serious, scared, tears pool in her eyes. Since her mom was killed when she was a baby, Tarek has been her only parent. Now Tarek is gone. Of course, she is terrified of being abandoned again.

"When is my dad coming back?" she asks softly.

"I don't know. Greg and Stevie went looking for him." Vega won't lie to her and tell her all will be fine. What could drive Tarek away from Eleni? Lin indicated Daniel. What happened between those three? Did Tarek stomp off in anger, and then was kidnapped by those Neo-Nazis?

Eleni hangs her head. Vega looks down at the forest floor too.

"Look, Eleni." They crouch down together and examine blades of grass growing out of a rock; ants building their empire, crawling in and out of their anthill carrying heavy loads; mushrooms standing in groups jointly digesting a moldy pine branch. "They look like long-legged party guests at a cocktail party."

Eleni smiles a little when Vega tells her about the party guests.

One thing feeds on the other, as plants and animals transform from one manifestation into another. The answer to all questions is metabolism, or metamorphosis from one form of life to another. Vega likes the idea that the components making up her body will one day be part of the blue blossoms of a mountain lupine, or the shimmering feathers of a blue jay. Nothing is lost, nothing is wasted. She doesn't have to worry and hold on so tight to her ego, her identity, her opinions. *A comforting thought that we are not that important. None of us is.*

Vega doesn't tell Eleni that. Instead, she teaches her the song of the free wild bird that sits on its branch all night singing. It's a song her German mother taught her when she was a child, and one she sang to her sons when they were young.

Eleni smiles as she hums along to the refrain *"Ich bin ein frei wild Vögelein und niemand kann mich zwingen."* The blue jay perches above them on a shrub oak branch, not joining in, but maybe listening, and obviously feeling safe enough to stay.

LIN:

Lin is outside watering the vegetable garden. The potatoes they planted are growing quickly. Stevie and Greg went into town to speak to the sheriff. Snatches of a song float up from the hillside below her. Lin picks up her sword and practices underneath the deck. She swings her katana through the air like a baton in a marching band. Daniel should practice with his bow and arrow, but he's inside with Rose. Lin refuses to speak to him.

"Where is Eleni?" Lin hears Rose's voice from the living room.

"She was just here a minute ago," Daniel assures her.

"But now she's gone!"

"Midnight is with her," Daniel says. "I'm sure they just went for a little walk. But I'll go check on them."

"For a walk? How can they go for a walk? It's dangerous out there. The forest is no place for a little girl!"

"I can hear her singing," Inge calls in from the deck.

"What is she singing?"

"It's a German song," Inge explains. "About a free, wild bird."

"It's the song my mom used to sing to me at bedtime," Daniel says.

"How can she sing at a time like this? She's just drawing attention to herself. This forest is crawling with Neo-Nazis!"

"What do you mean, Rose? What are you talking about?" Daniel's voice sounds sharp.

Lin wonders if Rose heard about the body.

"Well," backpedaling now, "they are all over this area, hunting."

"Why do you think the poachers were Neo-Nazis, Rose? What gave you that idea?" Daniel says.

Rose's answer sounds tentative. "Because they are all over. They are the real threat."

Daniel doesn't answer, but Lin wonders about Rose's sources of information.

. . .

GREG:

At the Black Market behind the church, all they get in exchange for five bottles of fine wine and water are two young chickens and a bag of potatoes. Greg's not pleased. It's getting harder and harder to get supplies. Fine wine is a luxury people can do without. They stop by Patrick's table of books. "How was that champagne?" Greg asks.

"Excellent. I drank it right away. I'm not keeping anything valuable around."

"Why's that?"

Patrick nods toward the Bastards at the periphery of the market. "They plunder everything. Caravans of refugees have started to come to Juniper, looking for water, for food, for safety. The Bastards take whatever they want. Nobody can stand up to them. See all the stuff they have?"

"We have seen the camp down at the lake. It's already overflowing," Stevie says.

"That's why they come here. It's a few more hours walking uphill, but they are desperate."

Tables are heaped with jackets, boots, and hats in front of the Bastards. Where are all the former owners of these items, Greg wonders.

"Ironically, I've been spared, since the Bastards are not interested in books," Patrick says with a rueful smile.

"The sheriff?" Stevie asks.

Patrick just shakes his head. "Take this," he presses a book into Stevie's hands. "It may come in handy."

Stevie thanks him and as they walk away, he reads the title to Greg.

"*The Art of War,* by the 5th Century BC Chinese military strategist Sun Tzu. Cool."

"Read fast, Stevie. We need all the help we can get. The sheriff will show up at the cabin soon to snoop around. We need to prepare. We have to convince the sheriff we're living in a defendable fortress." Greg doesn't want Sheriff Baker to tell the Superior Bastards that they only have four men and six women at the cabin.

WHEN THEY GET BACK, the cabin doesn't look anything like a defensible space. Colorful laundry flutters off the metal wire on the deck's banisters. The women have attached it with wooden laundry pins. It looks like Tibetan prayer flags or a festive party decoration. Not the impression they are aiming for.

Greg sighs. "Stevie, what are your plans for the fortification?"

"Metal, dad. We have left-over roofing panels downstairs, and I want to line the deck with them to create a battlement. It's much better protection than plywood, I tested it. And it's low enough to look over."

"Good. The sheriff will assume we're either holding Jack Smith or that we killed him."

"Whoever killed him, did what had to be done," Stevie says.

Greg looks at his son in profile. "Why would you say that? We have no idea who killed Jack."

"I just thought ..." Stevie stammers.

"Don't make any assumptions until we know what happened."

Stevie bites his lip.

Greg parks the car in the driveway and they get out. Stevie disappears below the deck. The garage door is wide open. Greg's disabled SUV is parked face out. Hilde and Inge are sitting in the front seats of the car, nodding to fifties pop songs. Greg looks at them with consternation and walks up to the driver's side.

He leans into the window. "What are you guys doing here?"

"We had to get away from the wrath of Rose," Hilde stage-whispers, winking at him with her bright blue eyes. "Daniel showed us how to listen to a playlist on this little speaker. What a fabulous invention. It plays music from our youth!"

"Are you drinking again?" Greg asks the two stationary passengers with a wink.

"Oh, no," Hilde says and tries to hide something on her lap.

"What do you have there?"

"Swiss chocolate. Would you like some?" Hilde asks in her most charming voice.

"You still have chocolate?"

"I brought some in my bag. I'm sorry we didn't share." Hilde quickly turns off the speaker, and suddenly there is silence.

Greg turns around to unload the potatoes. Inge lowers her hand, which was halfway up to her mouth with a piece of chocolate.

"How did it go?" Vega joins them from the house.

"We made some flyers and the sheriff said he would distribute them, but he didn't seem very concerned. Also, he's on his way up here. Looking for another missing man —one of the Bastards." Greg looks Vega straight in the eye, and she nods knowingly.

"Did you get any provisions at the Black Market?" she asks.

"Not much. A sack of potatoes. And a couple of young chickens. It's getting tough."

"I'll cook tonight," Hilde calls out from the car.

"What's going on with Rose and Hilde?" Greg asks Vega.

"Rose resents Hilde being here. It seems she has forgotten that this is our cabin, and Hilde is part of our family."

"I'll talk to Rose. She'll get over it."

"There are two chicks here!" Eleni cries with delight.

She discovered them in a box on the backseat of the Mustang.

"You want to help me build a chicken coop for them?" Greg asks.

"Yes, yes, let's build them a nice chicken house!"

STEVIE:

Approaching the cabin, Stevie sees Lin doing katana exercises below the deck. She looks like a Chinese Dragon princess, her long hair flying and her slim legs flexing. He goes below to join her.

"Looking good, Lin."

She smiles without interrupting her flow. He picks up his sword.

"Let's practice together. Upper left strike, upper right, block low, overhead strike, lower middle, and side swipe!" Their swords clang together as they complete the training sequence like a ballroom dance, circling around each other. They laugh and catch their breath. Stevie feels a lightheadedness he can only identify as joy.

"How'd it go in town?"

He shrugs. "The place is in shambles. Lots of desperate people picking through the trash, which nobody hauls away any more."

"I feel partially responsible," Lin is taking a swig of water from her pink bottle.

"For the lack of trash pick-up?"

"No, not for that. For Tarek running off."

"I thought Daniel said something to upset him,"

"He did, but it was in response to something I did."

Stevie sits down at the picnic bench and places his katana carefully on the table. "You shouldn't blame yourself. It was stupid of Tarek to run off. Now he's in big trouble and so are we."

"Tarek and I have something in common. We're both people of color. We know how it feels to be unwelcome."

"Has anybody made you feel unwelcome here?"

"No, not here."

"Everybody loves you. And Tarek is with Rose. If anybody is treated like she doesn't belong here, it's Hilde."

"I noticed that." Lin stares into the considerable distance. Stevie follows her gaze to the snow-covered San Jacinto Mountains in the north.

"Well, I'm very glad you're here," Stevie says and feels like a total idiot as soon as the words are out of his mouth. He hopes she's not going to take it the wrong way. He meant it as a compliment, but he's not really even sure what he actually meant to say, except that he finds her attractive, or lovely, admirable ... *This is so confusing.*

Lin doesn't answer. But she smiles. That's something. It's certainly better than getting mad at him.

14

DAY 43: STEVIE

Hilde makes spaghetti and tomato sauce. Stevie sits at the kitchen counter, reading his *Art of War* book.

"I think that's all she *can* cook," Rose says to Stevie behind her held-up hand from her seat at the table where she leafs through a very old *New Yorker Magazine*, looking at the cartoons.

Hilde makes a lot of noise clattering with the largest pot she can find.

"How many of these spaghetti packages should I use?" Hilde calls to Inge, who is also sitting at the table looking at a cook book.

"We're nine people, so maybe three packages?" Inge answers.

"Oh good, that's all we have anyway."

She dumps all the noodles into the pot before the water even boils.

"Our last packages!" Rose comments.

Hilde has opened a bottle of wine, and she and Inge toast each other.

"What's there to toast? Dumping Kraft spaghetti into a pot of cold water?" Rose mumbles

"Three cans of tomato sauce?" Hilde asks.

"Sure, if we have that many. I'll go and get some fresh herbs." Inge goes outside to the little herb garden to pick some rosemary and oregano.

"I'll go with you. Let's check on the chickens too." Eleni, who was sitting on the floor with Midnight, puts on her shoes and follows Inge outside.

"A little salt and pepper," Hilde chirps cheerfully.

"How many glasses of wine have you had?" Rose asks irritably.

Hilde ignores her. "Ooops, that's more than I intended," she tips the salt container over and spills its contents all over the kitchen counter. "Oh dear, Rose can you help me here?"

"No, I'm busy. I'm sure you can handle it."

Hilde sweeps piles of salt into the palm of her hand throws them into the trash.

"Doesn't she realize this might be the last salt we can get our hands on? Has she considered how we will manage when the salt is gone?" Rose says quietly in Stevie's direction. He turns the page on his book and tries to tune her out.

The water is boiling furiously. It foams and bubbles over the rim, spilling all over the stovetop.

"Where are Vega or Inge? Someone has to stop this disaster," Rose says louder now.

Hilde tries to lift the pot from the burner, but it is heavy, and she drops it again, spilling more. "Well, at least it's boiling." She turns off the burner and stirs the tomato sauce, which is also bubbling wildly and splattering red sticky drops on the wall, stove, and counter.

"Who's going to clean up this mess?" Rose says to no one in particular.

Eleni and Inge return with bundles of herbs. "They smell so good," Eleni holds a little bouquet of oregano up to Rose's nose.

The others come in.

"Dinner almost ready?" Greg asks.

"Eleni, can you set the table?" Inge asks while cleaning and chopping the herbs.

"Stevie, can you help me drain the spaghetti?" Hilde asks.

Stevie goes behind the counter and drains the pot into a colander. "Hilde, these are all clumped together. Didn't you stir them?" he asks.

"I must have forgotten. We'll have to cut them in slices, I suppose." She stares at the clump. "Can you help me serve?" She pleads and separates smaller clumps from the big one, which she piles on plates and smothers with sauce. Stevie carries them to the table.

"Guten Appetit!" Hilde says and lifts her glass.

Everybody stares at the heaps on their plates. Greg eats a mouthful of pasta mass with sauce. Puts the fork down. "What did you do, Hilde?"

"The salt kind of spilled, the top was open and I didn't realize ..."

"I can't eat this ..." Eleni says in a tiny voice.

"What have you done? You wasted precious resources on this inedible junk!" Rose's remark has the intended effect. Hilde hangs her head, tears in her eyes. Rose looks around the table. "Now do you realize what you have done by taking in this incompetent outsider?"

"She meant well ..." Vega says.

Of course, she makes excuses for Hilde and takes her side, Stevie thinks.

Greg walks over to the kitchen, looks at the pasta water sloshed on the stove, the splatters of tomato on the wall, trails of salt on the floor, and shakes his head. "I'll try to dilute the sauce and make some sort of lasagna out of this."

Stevie looks up from his plate. He's the only one who is eating. "It's not gourmet, but it fills the stomach. It's time you realize this not a vacation retreat in the mountains. We're under siege and we're fighting for our survival. Get over it and eat. Complaining and being sensitive is not going to get us through."

Daniel and Lin stop poking around on their plates and dutifully put a forkful of the unappetizing mush into their mouths. They know Stevie is right, they can't afford to squander food.

"In the meantime, we can be as kind as possible to each other," Vega says with a sideways glance at Rose.

"What do you expect me to do?" Rose shoots back. "Throw stones at the enemy while exchanging polite remarks?"

15

DAY 45: STEVIE

Stevie feels someone shaking him gently by the shoulders. Must be his mom.

"Wake up Stevie, the red light's blinking."

Greg and Stevie are up within seconds. Greg storms out the door. Stevie is right behind him, screaming "Battle stations!" at the top of his lungs. Daniel joins them sleepily. The three of them manage to fall into the triangle position they practiced to project strength. Greg carries his Glock, Stevie and Daniel hold the two rifles they confiscated from the trespassing hunters.

At the crest of the hill, a phalanx of Superior Bastards seven across stand in front of their vintage army vehicle, weapons drawn. The two parties come to a stand-off about fifteen feet apart. Stevie notices one of the Bastards is a girl with long dreadlocks, dressed in torn black jeans and combat boots.

"This is our property line," Greg says. "Come any closer and we shoot. There are snipers in the house."

An empty threat, but his father wants to intimidate them in case they try to take them out.

Blackbeard, in the middle of the line, nods toward Greg. "So, we meet again."

Greg says, "I told you before not to come back."

Blackbeard seems to be their leader. He shakes his head. "The situation has changed. We have your man, Tarek."

Greg nods. "We figured. We demand his immediate release."

Blackbeard chuckles. "You are not really in a situation to make demands."

"What do you want?" Greg asks. Stevie realizes now comes the negotiation stage.

Blackbeard takes his time. Looks around. "Nice place you have here. Defensible, an alarm system, solar panels, water, a vegetable garden. Everything we need."

"Let's get to the point. As you said, the place is defensible."

"Your man Tarek. You can have him back in exchange for our man Jack."

"We want proof of life."

"He's alive, but not feeling too happy. Amy, show 'em."

The girl steps forward and throws a small plastic bag onto the road in the space between them.

"Stevie, pick it up."

Stevie crouches forward to get the bag, but never lets the Bastards out of his sight. The bag contains a polaroid of Tarek and a left pinky finger.

"Oh my God," Daniel exclaims when he sees the bloody stump.

"A non-fatal wound. Nobody really needs that last link of the little finger," Blackbeard says with a cruel smile.

"As I told you before, we don't have your Jack." Greg counters.

"Too bad for Tarek. We know Jack was headed this way. He never came back."

Stevie's mind is spinning. How are they going to get out of this predicament?

"If he is still here, we'll find him. Give us a few of days. We'll get back to you."

"Four days is all Tarek has."

The Bastards move backward toward their vehicle, but not before Blackbeard spits on the ground, and makes an expansive gesture toward the property, "Really nice set-up you have here." His eyes are narrow, greedy slits taking it all in.

16

DAY 48: TAREK

It's been a week since Tarek was kidnapped by the Superior Bastards, but it feels like an eternity. He's on his knees scrubbing the floor of the men's bathrooms, in the Old Theatre, where they are holed up. He's trying not to gag from the filth and the stink. Due to the water shortage, they make him use bleach, which burns his skin and eyes. The Bastards treat him like an animal, taunt him about his brown skin and Muslim religion. Once in a while they throw some food at him, just like they throw it to their two pit bulls. Those dogs frighten Tarek as much, if not more, than the men. The cut on his left hand is wrapped in a dirty bandage. He's worried it will get infected and fester.

When he ran away from Lin and Daniel, he just

wanted to blow off steam, get away from the judgment as an unwanted refugee, that follows him wherever he goes. But when he reached the paved road, a large military vehicle swerved in front of him. Two guys in army fatigues jumped down. One of them looked familiar. Both carried machine guns.

"Hey, I know this guy," the man with the black beard called. "He belongs to the ranch over here on Kosmik Mountain."

"An Arab?" the other man says.

"Yeah, can you believe it?"

"Let's grab 'em."

Tarek remembers the shock and the fear that paralyzed him. His heart beat in this throat, but his legs did not move. They bundled him in the truck, gagged him and tied him up. One of the men put a bag over his head. He'll never forget the terror of that car ride, blind-folded and afraid for his life. Not again, he thought. The ride through Bulgaria in a dark truck bed during his escape from Syria with Eleni came back with terrifying clarity.

The ride was short but felt endless. An abrupt stop threw him against the side of the truck. After the doors opened, he was pulled roughly from the vehicle and dragged into a building. Inside they tied him to a pipe before they removed the bag from his head. He found himself in utility room, full of pipes, tanks and tools— sadly far out of his reach. For the past week, he's been treated like a slave forced to work eighteen hours a day for the Bastards.

But once the Bastards sleep, Amy comes and brings him tea, food, and herbal compresses for his bruises. She has long, brown dreadlocks and huge hazelnut eyes. Her face looks dark, but Tarek is not sure if it just looks like that in the dim light or if it is dirty. She moves smoothly, quietly like a cat when she comes to him at night. He asks her why she was kind to him. "Don't you have anywhere else to go? You must be really desperate to stay with these Bastards."

"I have no other place to go. It's a cold and tough world out there for a girl on her own," she says. "Who'd take me in? Everybody is desperate. And the Bastards would destroy anybody foolish enough to give me shelter. Did you see how many weapons they have?"

Tarek hasn't seen the weapons, but he believes her. He thinks of his daughter, Eleni. It pains him to imagine how upset she must be since he disappeared. He wonders if Greg is looking for him. Why would he? Tarek's a stranger. He was not wanted at the cabin in the first place. Without him, there's one less mouth to feed.

"Don't you have any family?" he asks Amy.

"No, my mother is gone." Amy says sharply.

"Where did you live?"

"We lived in a small house at the edge of town. We were pretty isolated and an easy target for looters after the solar storm. No more questions."

Tarek wonders if Amy's mother died during the attack.

Amy visits every night. She's his only comfort here. A sympathetic ear and a shoulder to lean on. Someone who treats him humanely, not like a beast. And Tarek tries to do the same for her.

17

DAY 49: GREG:

The alarm system's loud ring signals a new arrival. The sheriff's black-and-white patrol car comes to a halt at the crest of the hill. Greg goes out to meet him. Stevie and Daniel follow. They stop eight feet away from the police car, standing in a line across the dirt road, and watch the portly sheriff climb out with grunts and groans.

"Sheriff," Greg says. "You met my son, Stevie. This is my older son, Daniel."

The sheriff tips his hat.

"We have proof that Tarek has been captured by the Superior Bastards," Greg says.

"What proof?" the sheriff asks with an inscrutable expression.

"They delivered a piece of his finger and a polaroid

showing him tied-up on a chair in what looks like the Old Theatre."

"Hmpf. I searched the old theater and didn't see him." The sheriff pulls up his pants, which sag underneath his bulging belly.

"They issued demands."

"Did they now?" the sheriff drawls.

So far nobody has moved. It's not like they want to invite him in. The women and Eleni are hiding in the dugout.

"We can't meet their demands."

"These are desperate times." The sheriff shrugs.

"Is that all you have to say? We know Tarek is a kidnap victim in the Old Theater. Isn't it your job to get him back?"

"First let me look around your property for a member of the Bastards, Jack Smith. They believe you are holding him here."

"They want this Jack in exchange for Tarek. But we can't give anything back we don't have."

The sheriff walks toward them and there's nothing else to do but step back. Approaching the cabin, he studies the metal barricades around the deck.

"Are you expecting somebody?" the sheriff asks.

"We are ready to defend ourselves," says Stevie.

The sheriff raises his eyebrows. "Hmpf," he says again.

"You really think we are holding this Jack in our cabin?

Feel free to search. We have nothing to hide." Greg gestures toward the entrance door.

"Let's go and see," the sheriff says.

Greg walks ahead and opens the front door. The cabin has an open floor plan. Walking in, they stand immediately in the large main room, the kitchen separated only by a wide island with a granite countertop. There's a wooden stove in one corner, and the big table in front of the picture window. No place to hide. On either side of the main room, a door leads to the two bedrooms. The sheriff takes a step into each room and peeks into the adjoining bathrooms while Greg and the boys watch.

"Okay, let me see the basement," Sheriff Baker says.

They climb down the outside stairs alongside the house to the basement level. Most of the supplies have been moved to the dugout. It's dark in the basement, and they have created as much clutter as possible with of scraps of wood, rolls of tarpaper, and chicken wire arranged to create an obstacle course. Daniel and Lin's cot has been dismantled and loaded with tools. They don't want the sheriff to think, that they are holding Jack as prisoner down here.

"What a mess," Sheriff Baker pokes about aimlessly, climbs over sawhorses, peers under a dark workbench, and stumbles into a weed whacker.

"It's just a storage area," Greg says.

"Is this all the food you have left?" the sheriff asks.

"We're running low. So, what are you going to do about Tarek?"

"Let's see the rest of the property," the sheriff says.

"Okay." Greg leads the way down the steepest path to the edge of the cleared land, where they quickly encounter dense brushwork. After a few steps, the sheriff predictably begins to huff and puff, gasping for air.

"How far down does it go?"

"We own twenty acres, all the way to the Indian reservation. We haven't been able to clear the brush yet beyond this point." Greg points to the steep drop-off two hundred meters ahead down a slippery slope.

The sheriff takes a few more tentative steps. "I've seen enough," he announces. "I'll go tell the Bastards you don't have Jack and to let your Tarek go."

18

DAY 50: TAREK

Tarek's hands are handcuffed to a pipe, and he's crouched on the bare, cold floor in a back corner of the old theatre. It's the middle of the night, but it's impossible to sleep. He's exhausted from a day of chopping wood, cleaning toilets, and burning trash. His head hurts from dehydration, hunger, and the blow from Blackbeard's—he still doesn't know his real name— baseball bat. His left hand throbs where they cut off his little finger, and blood still seeps through.

He would have given up long ago if it weren't for Amy. He's still in disbelief that she helps him; that she doesn't look down on him like everybody else. She's his only ally in this God-forsaken place. Probably because she's little more than a slave herself. The Bastards use her as cook, cleaner, and maid. When he asked, if they raped her, she emphatically shook her head, but didn't explain why not.

Her bare feet tiptoe toward him. As soon as the Bastards are out cold, she comes to him. She puts a chamomile compress on his head and changes his bandage. He sighs with relief. The smell of the herbs she applies is as soothing as her gentle hands. She brought a cheese sandwich and a water bottle, and helps him to eat and drink since his hands are tied. They huddle together under the blanket she tucks around them, and she is resting her head on his shoulder. He feels her body relax and hopes she is getting a little sleep.

"I have a plan how we can get out of here," she whispers in his ear.

Tarek turns his head so he can see her face. "How? Did you find the key to unlock my handcuffs?"

"I know where it is. The real challenge are the dogs."

The pair of pit bulls, growling, drooling, straining at their leashes, scare the hell out of Tarek. The dogs would raise alarm if they tried to get out.

"How are we going to silence them?"

"With a long knife."

He lets out a sharp breath. "I was hoping for something a bit more subtle."

"We're way past subtle." Amy shakes her head. Her clumped dreadlocks move against his shoulder. Her threadbare sweater is barely held in place with strips of fabric and bands of cloth. Her pants are tied at the waist with a piece of rope. The soles of her shoes are half detached and leave a gaping hole at the front. This girl needs to get out of here even more than he. Unlike her, he has a place to go. When he told her about the cabin, she thought it sounded like Nirvana.

"Even if we can kill the dogs, and you can unlock my handcuffs, we still won't get far without shoes. It's at least ten miles from here to the cabin."

"Ten miles is nothing," Amy says. "We can get there in four hours."

Her voice is raspy and rough from a chronic dry cough.

He turns to look at her. Can he just bring her to the cabin? What would the others think? Another stranger? Her dirty face blends in with the dark surroundings, but her eyes shine white in the darkness. In daylight they're as blue as the spring sky, only more radiant. There's no way he'd leave her behind.

"I don't even know the way back from here. But even without the dogs, the cabin is going to be the first place they'll look for us."

"I know the way to Kosmik Mountain. Your people will help us, won't they?"

"Of course." Actually, Tarek is not so sure about that. Will they even have enough for another mouth to feed?

"I can't wait to take a shower and burn these clothes." She laughs her throaty laugh.

Someone stirs in the main hall of the theater, where

the Bastards are sleeping. Tarek freezes. He hears the creaking floorboards and slow, groggy steps of a sleepy man. Too late for Amy to steal away. If the Bastards find them together, they'll both be beaten with the horsewhip. A door squeaks. A log of wood is thrown into the stove with a hissing sound. The stove door closes, and the steps retreat to a mattress on the floor.

Amy's shoulders drop in relief, and Tarek lets out a long breath he didn't know he had been holding.

"We have to go soon. I can't take it anymore."

He nods. "Tomorrow night."

19

DAY 51: TAREK

Tarek props the ax between his legs and tries to rub some feeling into his freezing hands. His last day with the Superior Bastards if all goes according to plan. He's in front of the Old Theatre, chopping wood. The Bastards have felled most of the ancient pine trees at the site and it is his job to cut the trunks down to size for their wood stove. A cold spell has descended over Juniper, and the apple blossoms are dying.

Johnny sits on a stump, supervising. One of the two pit bulls, the one with the black eye, who looks like he's just been punched in the face, lies at Johnny's feet. The dog's called Goering, after Hitler's designated successor, and even though he's lying down he does not look relaxed. The dog watches every move Tarek makes, and once in a while he flexes his powerful chest muscles in a show of force. Goering and Johnny are inseparable.

Johnny sips coffee from a tin mug. Tarek can see the steam rising in the cold morning air.

"Just keep chopping and you'll feel warmer soon," Johnny is wrapped in a warm parka.

Wow, what great advice! Easy for Johnny to say. Tarek drops his head and studies the rags wrapped around his raw, blistered fingers.

"Alright," Johnny says and hands him a pair of gloves. "Maybe the work will go faster with these."

Tarek looks Johnny in the eye in a silent acknowledgment of this small act of kindness.

"I used to do this work before you came," Johnny says. "I know how it feels."

"Oh yeah?" Tarek keeps chopping. It's my last day, he thinks with each blow of the ax.

"I used to be the underdog around here," Johnny adds.

Tarek's less than the underdog. He's a captive held against his will, forced into labor, but to keep Johnny talking he asks "How's that?"

"Look at me." Johnny opens his arms to present his skinny body. "I'm small, I'm young and I had no experience with their right-wing ideology before I came here. I was just a lost boy."

Tarek estimates Johnny is no older than sixteen and the dog seems to be his only companion here. Maybe that's why he's opening up to him. Who else does he have? "Where're you from?" he asks.

"Jacumba, out east in the desert. I don't do well in the cold."

"What happened to your family?" Whack, two perfectly split halves of wood fall on each side of the chopping block.

"We lived in a trailer park, my mom, dad and brother. The solar storm set it on fire. All the electric wiring was jury-rigged. The fire killed our parents. So, my brother and I packed up whatever we could and joined a caravan to the coast."

"On foot?"

Johnny nods. "Along the way we took whatever we could to stay alive."

"What happened to your brother?"

"Shot in a liquor store. These guys took me in because I was small and fast and good at stealing."

"Why are you telling me all this?"

"You gave me one of the turkeys up on your hill."

The front door of the theater opens and Blackbeard appears in the doorframe. "What are you guys chatting about? This is no cocktail party. Get some wood over here. It's cold inside."

"Coming," Johnny shouts and stacks wooden logs in a metal bin. "Goering, you watch Tarek here while I'm inside," he commands. Goering growls in Tarek's direction. He listens to every word Johnny says.

It's your last day here too, Goering. Tarek feels a pang of regret, but the dog's not his friend.

Amy comes out carrying a heavy metal bucket filled with ash from the fireplace. Her face and hair are dotted with gray ash flakes. She looks at him and mouths "Tonight!"

He nods. Johnny comes back and throws a piece of meat to Goering, who snatches it up with his powerful jaws.

"Here," Johnny hands Tarek half a sandwich; white bread with some unidentifiable canned meat.

"Thanks."

"Just eat it, you know, with your back to the door."

Tarek wolfs down the sandwich. Who knows when he will get anything else?

The town of Juniper is still quiet and empty at this time of the morning. Fog hangs heavy between the pines on this side of the road leading to Main Street. All he hears are drops of condensation falling from pine needles, and the blow of his ax as it splits another log—until the fog carries the sound of shuffling feet in his direction. Many feet on wet asphalt, heavy breathing, and suppressed groans. Johnny hears it too. Goering gets to his feet with his ears pointing straight up like small antennae.

Johnny whistles toward the house. "Another caravan," he calls.

The people in the caravan must have walked all night to get here so early. Tarek can imagine their exhaustion and despair, having been a refugee on the run himself. Within minutes, six Bastards armed with firearms and bats exit the theater and trot toward Main Street. A caravan means warm clothes, boots, food and who knows what else these desperate refugees have been able to salvage and carry all the way up here.

The remaining Bastards position themselves in the windows and on the roof to defend the compound. Tarek squeezes his eyes shut and wishes he could close his ears as well. He doesn't want to see and hear what's going to happen next.

STEVIE:

Greg called a family meeting on the deck. They sit in a circle.

"The Superior Bastards have Tarek. They won't give him up until we meet their demands."

Stevie's mind flashes to the moment they dropped Jack's body over the cliff.

"Whatever it takes, we need to get him back," Rose says tearfully.

"Yes, Rose, but don't you want to know their demand first? We all have to agree, because it will have a significant impact on all of us."

"Why?" Rose asks.

"They want Jack back." Stevie says.

"Who is Jack?"

"You might as well tell them," Vega says.

Greg sighs. Stevie and Lin grit their teeth.

"I found a dead body on the path up to Kosmik Peak a few weeks ago," Greg says grudgingly, looking at Vega for help. "Turns out he was one of the Bastards, called Jack."

"Greg hid the body to protect us," Vega says.

Rose, Inge, gasp. Hilde's eyes widen and her face turns red. Eleni bursts into tears, until Vega puts her arm around her and pulls her close.

"What do you mean by 'hid?' You got rid of a dead body?" Rose shouts.

"His body is in the ravine," Lin says. "Could we even get him out of there?"

"If it brings back Tarek …" Rose says hopefully.

"You really think returning a murdered member to those Neo-Nazis will appease them?" Stevie asks sharply.

"He was murdered?" Rose asks. "That's a little detail you left out."

Stevie didn't mean to let that detail slip out.

"So, now you know. How do you want to proceed?" Greg asks.

"It's impossible to give them what they want," Stevie says.

Most people around the circle nod in agreement, with the exception of Rose.

"But what else can we do?" she wails.

"Negotiate," Greg's suggests. "Offer them something else they want. Find a compromise."

"But they already steal whatever they want from the townspeople and the caravans." Stevie's thinking of the piled high tables at the Black Market.

"We could offer them another hostage. I'll go in exchange for Tarek," Greg offers.

"Absolutely not," Vega protests and grabs Greg's hand as if she'd never let it go.

Stevie can't believe Greg would even consider abandoning them.

"No way," Inge protests.

"It's a noble offer, but it wouldn't solve anything. Even if they agreed, we'd just exchange one hostage for another," Lin says, and everybody nods.

"I'd have a better chance to escape. I'll go prepared." Greg sounds confident, but Stevie wonders if he's just trying to reassure them.

"How about finding allies. We need help. How about neighbors? Townspeople?" Hilde asks.

Greg shakes his head. "The closest neighbors are the squatters down by the lake. And the townspeople are too afraid."

"What about the county sheriff? There must be some agency we could go for help. They can't all be corrupt," Inge suggests.

"I've been monitoring the emergency broadcasts," Daniel says. "Looting and violence is rampant everywhere. There aren't enough law enforcement officers to maintain order. The few that are left are not paid or supervised. I heard many reports about corrupt police forces. It will be months, if not years, before we get any assistance up here." Daniel and Lin sit hand in hand.

Stevie is relieved they have made up their differences. The last thing he wants right now is tension between him and his brother. "What broadcasts?" Stevie asks.

"There are a few people with short-wave radios. Others like us, who have functioning solar power and are not completely cut off from the world. Mostly preppers who expected some kind of apocalypse based on right-wing conspiracy theories."

"Good job, Daniel. Keep us posted." Greg says.

"All that talking isn't getting us anywhere," Stevie says. "Let's confront the Bastards in their den. Maybe we can get a glimpse of Tarek. Assess their defenses. See, if there's a way to break him out of there."

"I like that idea," Lin says. "But don't let them know Jack is dead. They'll assume we killed him."

"They are more likely to listen to us, if we offer them something valuable in return for Tarek." Daniel says. "We don't have to go through with it."

Vega turns to Greg. "Every confrontation carries a risk. You might be killed, wounded, captured, all for nothing. They outnumber us, have more weapons."

"Vega is right," Hilde says. "We don't want anybody else get hurt. How about going to the sheriff again?"

Rose turns on her, "You are so self-centered, Hilde.

They cut off Tarek's finger. What would you want us to do if they kidnapped you?"

Eleni starts crying again.

Greg looks at her. "Eleni needs her father. We can't abandon Tarek. I'll leave Stevie and Daniel in case you have to defend yourselves without me. I'll ask the sheriff to come with me. Tell him I want to negotiate."

"Thank you, Greg," Rose looks up at her brother tearfully.

Greg waits for further comments. "Can we have a vote? All in favor?"

Vega votes against the plan, but the ayes have it. Stevie doesn't want Greg to go by himself. He takes him aside. "Dad, take me with you."

"No, Stevie, you're needed here. It's better if I go alone. Trust me." Greg turns away to get ready. He leaves the two rifles with Stevie and Daniel, and keeps his Glock. Stevie stops him, as Greg hands him one of the confiscated weapons. "Dad, please ..." He feels abandoned by his father, as if he were a little boy again, sent to summer camp on his own.

"Steven, I trust you to protect your mother and your family," Greg says gravely and looks him in the eye. Stevie swallows and nods.

"You know how to handle this, right Daniel?" Greg asks his older son.

"We practiced, but I never fired a bullet because we have to save ammunition."

"You'll do fine." Greg hugs his sons and wife good-bye.

VEGA:

Vega watches Greg drive off, and wonders if she'll ever see him again. What would they do without him? What would *she* do without him? They shouldn't have let him go. He's the most indispensable person here. She gets up to run after him, but there's only a small cloud of dust left behind in his wake.

Above her, clouds are piled up in the sky as if someone had thrown them together in a rush. They move quickly, changing shapes and color, from white to gray.

It all escalated so quickly after Greg found Jack's dead body on the trail. Why did he ever come here. Was he the root cause? They're still no closer to knowing what happened. Normally, Greg and her are able to investigate a murder. This time they are just swept up in the unfolding events, and seem to have no control over what happens. She knows that's hard for Greg. Hopefully, he won't take any unnecessary risks. The least she can do is take the watch on the log overlooking the entrance to the compound, anxious to be the first one to identify who is coming over the crest of the road.

It seems like Vega listened for hours to the chirps of birds and rustling of leaves in the trees. Until finally the roar of a car approaches. Stevie appears in the cabin's doorway, waiting for her signal to go to battle stations. The engine comes closer and the red Mustang emerges over the hill. Thumbs up! Stevie nods and runs to greet the arrival.

They all surround the car in the driveway as it comes to a stop and Greg climbs out. Thank God, he's unharmed. Vega runs to him and embraces him.

Greg looks over Vega's shoulder. "You want the good news or the bad news?" Greg asks.

"Good news," Rose says as Vega steps back.

"The good news is I'm alive and back safely. The bad news is, that we have no deal. The sheriff is dead. I found him shot in his office. The Bastards gave us one more day to meet their demands and then they'll cut off Tarek's body parts."

"Oh, my God," Rose grabs Greg's arm. "Did you see him?"

"I saw him through a window. Someone held a gun to his head. They have an incentive to keep him alive until we meet their demands. They just laughed when I offered to take Tarek's place."

"We can't give Jack back." Vega is shaking with released tension and rising dread.

"They seem to have given up on Jack. Now they want this ranch—the supplies, the land, the solar system, the water, everything. We would be relegated to the basement, basically as prisoners in our own home and under their command."

"Impossible! Never!" Stevie shouts. The others grumble and mutter among themselves.

"But if it brings Tarek back ..." Rose pleads tearfully, eyes wide with panic.

"You're okay with sleeping in the basement, no shower, no toilet and sharing the kitchen and bathrooms with the Bastards, if they even let you in?" Stevie says sharply.

"Tarek wouldn't be any better off. We'd all be captives. They could torture and maim any of us to control the others," Lin says.

"What else can we do?" Rose wails.

"Build our defenses." Greg says.

Stevie nods, so do Lin, and Daniel. Vega looks pained and undecided.

Eleni starts to cry. "What's going to happen to my dad?"

Rose puts her arm around her. "Yes, what's going to happen to him? Are you going to sacrifice him?" she shouts at Greg.

"He put himself in danger," Stevie says.

"You're only saying this because he is Syrian. You want to make Eleni an orphan? What if they had cut Hilde's finger off?" Rose is in hysterics now, and Eleni sobs uncontrollably.

"Hilde didn't run away and put us all in jeopardy." Stevie says coldly.

"Let's calm down everybody," Vega pleads. "There must be a way to rescue Tarek and protect ourselves. Eleni has a right to her father."

"What's your solution, mom?" Stevie glares at Vega. "A group meditation?"

"We have one day! We have to come up with a better plan." Vega says and tries to ignore Stevie's taunt.

"What can we do, dad?" Daniel faces his father.

"We're going to sleep on it."

20

DAY 52: TAREK

Tarek is waiting in the darkness for Amy. They'll either escape tonight or die trying. He hopes Amy won't have to die with him.

He saw Greg through the window earlier in the day. He knows Greg was bargaining for his release, but Tarek has no illusions. Blackbeard sharpened his hunting knife in front of him. Asked him, if he was right- or left-handed. His only hope is to escape tonight.

Finally, he hears steps approaching. But the steps sound like heavy boots approaching on the wooden floor, not Amy's padded feet. Did something go wrong? He envisions the Bastards discovering their plan. Did they catch Amy and now they are coming for him? He thinks of Eleni. Stops breathing—as if that was going to help.

"Tarek?"

Amy's voice. Thank God. He dares to breathe again.

"Here." She kneels behind him and unlocks his hand-cuffs. He rubs his sore wrists. "You scared me. Where'd you get the boots?"

"Johnny gave them to me. They're from the caravan. They were too small for him."

They both fall silent. It's not like the caravan is a store where you go and buy ladies' shoes. He and Eleni could have ended up in a caravan—once they ran out of food and water. No point dwelling on that now. "Let's take care of the dogs."

"Already done." She smiles and he holds her in his arms, now that his arms are finally free.

"You shouldn't have had to do that alone."

"It's okay. I found a better way to deal with the dogs and put the Bastards to sleep at the same time." She speaks in her normal raspy voice. No whispering tonight.

"How?"

"When I took the garbage out back today, I noticed a bush of blooming angel trumpet flowers."

"So?"

"They are part of the nightshade family, datura. They're highly toxic."

"You poisoned them?" He can't believe how pleased she sounds. He swallows hard. Now's no time to argue.

"I mixed the extract of the plant into the dogs' water

bowls, and into the Bastards' food. They're all out for the count."

"Are they going to die?"

"Not necessarily." Amy nods tightly. "The dogs probably won't make it, but the Bastards will come around eventually. They'll throw up a lot and have some bizarre hallucinations. But enough talk. Let's go. We have no time to lose. I heard them talking about cutting off your hand. We have a long way ahead of us."

Tarek shudders. First his hand, then what? His arm?

Amy pulls him up and pushes a pair of boots toward him. From the caravan, he assumes. She has a backpack ready with food and water.

They tiptoe through the theater. Tarek sees the dogs lying on the kitchen floor. Drool is dribbling out of Goering's mouth. Just as Tarek steps over him, the dog lets out a low growl.

"He's still alive," Tarek whispers to Amy.

"Let's go," she pulls his sleeve.

Goering opens his mouth and snaps at Tarek's leg. He groans and moves away. The dog can only move his head, but he bites down hard. A piece of Tarek's pants are in Goering's powerful jaw. He won't let go. He shakes his head and Tarek loses his balance. Amy kicks the dog in the neck. He whimpers and opens his mouth, but Tarek falls, crashing into the wall.

"Jesus, Tarek, let's get out of here."

One of the Bastards on the ground wakes up and vomits. He's moaning and they have to step over him. He grabs Amy's ankle. "Are you a demon or are you a devil?" he drawls.

"I'm a demon and I'll kick you all the way to hell!" She makes true of her promise and but he holds on to her leg. Tarek hits the Bastard over the head with one of the wood logs he has split. The Bastard falls back, moaning. Blood streams from his forehead.

"The demons of hell are rising ..." another bastard cries in terror.

"You bet they are!" Amy tells him calmly and stomps on his hands. She has a knife in her hands. Tarek sees the white of her eyes gleaming with terrifying fury in the dark.

Making their way across the dark theater, yard by yard is an obstacle course of bodies sprawled on the ground, partially paralyzed, eyes wide open watching in horror whatever nightmare appears to them. Tarek stays clear of Amy's reach. She's in a place of rage, he doesn't want to enter.

A figure suddenly looms over them, its shadow amplified by the weak moonlight from the window. His arms lift high over his head. He appears like a giant, closing in on them.

"Run," Amy whispers, but she can't move. They are both hypnotized by the approaching monster.

Tarek can see the black beard as the figure sways from side to side. It's their leader, the strongest and biggest of the Bastards. "Amy, snap out of it. We need to go!"

The figure takes a swipe at them with a pipe.

Tarek grabs the end of the pipe and pushes it away.

"I don't fear the fires of hell," the figure growls. He leans over and opens the wood-burning stove, reaches in with his bare hands and pulls out a smoldering log.

He throws the log in their direction. It slithers over the floor hitting one of the dark shapes on the ground. There is a spark and a crackle as the clothes of the figure on the ground catch fire. Blackbeard grabs another log and takes a big step closer. He swipes at Tarek, who ducks. Takes aim at Amy who pulls out her knife.

"You can't fight the devil," she snarls, and throws the knife at Blackbeard.

Blackbeard howls, lunges at them, the knife stuck in his thigh. His scream galvanizes them forward. They leap toward the door, as flames lick across the thrashing bodies behind them.

The door is locked.

"We're trapped!" Amy screams.

"No, we're not," Tarek turns around, sprints to the woodpile next to the fire, ignoring Blackbeard, who's on the ground holding his leg. Tarek grabs the ax and runs back to Amy, jumping over writhing figures. He takes aim at the door and hacks at it, while Amy kicks as hard as she can.

THE DOOR GIVES WAY.

Tarek falls out the splintered opening and takes a deep breath of cool night air. His lungs are burning. Amy tumbles after him. They collapse in a heap. That was too close, but they're free. Nothing else matters right now. Breathing heavily, they run along the deserted road toward the short cut leading to the cabin.

"What a scene. What will happen to Johnny? Will he survive? He was not half bad." Tarek takes one look back at the burning theater.

"I don't know." Amy urges him on. "We need to take care of ourselves. Look forward—not back."

They turn off the paved road into a dirt path. She's right. Just put one foot in front of the other. Tarek feels tension draining out of his body. Amy next to him inhales deeply. He takes her hand.

"Thanks Amy, for all you did for me. Without you, I'd still be tied up at the pipe—possibly missing another body part."

"Without you I wouldn't have anywhere to go. You have a home. A safe place." Amy's voice sounds scratchy and matter of fact.

"Is that why you helped me?" Of course, how could he

have been so stupid. She just needs a place to go. She's desperate. Everyone is.

"No, Tarek, I did feel sorry for you." She hesitates, looks at him. "And I—I like you."

He lets go of her hand. She felt sorry for him. Now that they are on the run, she tells him. All the nights she came to him, they sat in the dark holding each other. It was never about him. She was using him, just as he is using Rose. Without Rose, he wouldn't have a place to stay for him and Eleni either.

"Come on Tarek. Don't sulk. We made it. We're free."

"We have a long way to go, Amy." His voice comes out reserved, reproachful.

She scoffs. "What's your problem, Tarek?"

He swallows. Looks at the dark silhouette of the trees. Tries not to be sensitive. "I'm disappointed." Why does he feel disappointed? He's going back to Rose and Eleni. They must be desperate with worry. What did he expect from Amy? He expected a bit of respect.

"Look, we hardly know each other."

Amy walks faster and he has to hurry to keep up. "What do you want to know?

"Tell me about your parents," she asks.

"My father was an engineer in Syria, like me. He got killed by a bomb attack in 2012, a year after the civil war began."

"I'm sorry. I never knew my dad. My mom didn't want

to talk about him. She said he wasn't important. I have no idea what kind of person he was."

"My father was a good man."

"At least you knew him."

"I live with the pain of losing him." All his life he wanted to make his father proud. But he died before Tarek got his engineering degree. Felt cheated out of having him at his graduation. Seeing him smile, feeling his father's hand on his shoulders. Probably better not to dwell on that now. "What happened to your mom?"

Amy inhales sharply and walks in silence for a few steps on the soft forest path. "My mom raised me at the edge of town, right next to the forest. She knew a lot about plants. She taught me about healing herbs, and mushrooms and, yes, poisonous plants. The Bastards burned our house down."

"You're a bit of a witch, and I mean that as a compliment."

"Do you really? I think you were shocked about the trumpet flowers."

"Kind of. I'm sorry about Johnny. He was the only one, besides you, who showed any kindness." Tarek hopes the dogs didn't suffer.

"Johnny couldn't be trusted. Whatever happened can't be helped. I did what was necessary for our survival."

The half-moon has come out from behind a cloud illuminating their path.

Changing the subject she asks, "Where's your mom?"

"Dead, as well as my wife."

"Your daughter is at the cabin?"

"I can't wait to see her. She's everything to me."

She takes a quick water break, and when she exhales, her breath is visible in the cold night air. "Do you know what happened to Jack? Is your family holding him on your mountain?"

"I don't know." Shit, according to what Greg told him, Jack's excursion onto the mountain did not end well.

"He was a good man. He's the reason the Bastards left me alone. I hope he's okay."

"Tell me about Jack."

"The Bastards think you killed him."

"We aren't murderers," he hopes.

"I bet you didn't think I was a murderer either, did you? People do what they have to in order to survive."

They walk for a few minutes in silence, while Tarek tries to process what Amy told him. Jack was the reason the Bastards left her alone. What does that mean?

"How did Jack protect you from the other Bastards?" he finally asks, but he already has a sinking feeling about it.

"I was his girl."

There it is. She was using him to find her lover. Holy shit. He can't bring this girl home. "So, you just used me to get to the cabin!"

Amy stops in her tracks. "No, Tarek. You have to believe me. I have no allegiance to the Bastards. If I was on their side, I wouldn't have had to do anything. They would have hacked you to pieces and then stormed the cabin. But I'm worried about Jack."

Tarek flinches. "I owe you my freedom, and I'm grateful, but you never really did it for my sake. I'm just another Arab to you." He doesn't care how he sounds. He needs to know.

"Oh Tarek, don't be ridiculous. Of course, I like you. You're a good man."

"Well, that makes me feel a lot better. So, what is it you want?"

"I want to know what happened to Jack, pure and simple."

"The family didn't kill him." Tarek takes a step away from her.

"Okay, good. Nothing to worry about."

Tarek hears a growling in the underbrush. Heavy branches crack. He and Amy stop in their tracks.

"Someone's following us," Tarek whispers.

Amy shakes her head and puts her finger on her mouth. "Shhh."

The rustling sounds come closer, someone is deliberately putting one foot gently onto the forest floor, then another, then another. Not feet—*paws*. The low growling again and a mountain lion, four times the size of Johnny's pit bull, breaks out of the dense bushes lining the path.

Tarek's first instinct is to run, but he remembers that's

the wrong move. He can never outrun this giant cat, whose powerful chest muscles ripple smoothly under the almond-colored fur at every step. He hears Amy gasp beside him.

"Don't run. Stand behind me," he hisses. She does and Tarek stretches up to his full six-foot height and lifts his arms overhead.

The mountain lion bares his sharp fangs and snarls. In the moonlight he sees her tensing her hind legs.

"Ahhh goo baackkk!" Tarek roars at the cat.

The cat's legs relax slightly. Tarek's heart beats in his throat as fast as never before.

"Ahhhhrg. I'm bigger than youuuu!"

The big cat closes its mouth. The pointed ears lay down on its forehead. The tail starts to whip back and forth. Her concentration is broken. She emits one more half-hearted growl, turns around and disappears back into the bushes with a last swish of her tail.

Tarek and Amy collapse onto the ground. All the air and energy seem to flow out of him. He kneels as Amy grabs his shoulders.

"You saved us, Tarek, you were great!" She looks him straight in the eye. "You were impressive, really! I couldn't have scared her away like you did," says Amy. "For one thing, I'm too short."

"Well, let's keep on going." Tarek stands and holds out a hand to pull Amy up. She lets him.

At the bottom of the valley, the path forks in two directions. In the pale moonlight they have a hard time distinguishing which will take them to the cabin.

"One way goes to the Indian reservation. We don't want to take that one." Amy says.

"I think we need to go left," Tarek decides. *Maybe I should lead her astray. Maybe I need to keep her away from the family.*

21

DAY 53: VEGA:

"Wake up, Greg." Vega shakes his shoulders.

"What is it? Something happen?"

"I can't sleep."

"Well, I can."

"What are we going to do about Tarek?"

"We're sleeping on it, remember? You always say, put it into the cosmic washing machine at night, and you may have a solution in the morning. Nothing we can do right now." He turns over on his other side and immediately begins to snore.

Vega lies in bed, wide awake, listening to the sounds of the night. A hooting owl, the rustle of the breeze, the wind chimes—a persistent knocking.

"Greg!"

"Vega, I really need my sleep."

"Someone's knocking at the door! Now they're knocking at the window!"

With one swift movement Greg is out of bed and at the door, Glock in hand. Vega's right behind him, hand on his back.

"It's me, Tarek," a subdued voice says. "Open up."

"Tarek?" Greg opens the door a crack, turns on the outside light. "Jesus, Tarek, come in." He pulls him inside. A young woman steps in with him.

Vega throws her arms around Tarek. "You're safe. How'd you get here?" Vega is so relieved to see him that she ignores the young woman at his side.

"By foot," he says.

Stevie joins them. "You really had us worried, especially Eleni." Stevie looks at the young woman standing silently behind Tarek.

"This is Amy." Tarek says. "Without her, I wouldn't be here. Hell, I probably wouldn't be alive."

"Thank you, Amy, for helping Tarek. I'm Vega."

STEVIE:

Amy looks familiar. Her long brown dreadlocks reach all the way down her back. Her clothes are tied together, bandaged in place. But she stands straight, with confidence. He's seen her before. At the stand-off with the

Bastards. She delivered their ultimatum and Tarek's finger.

"This is nice," she says, looking around. "Really nice. You have all this space, and a deck, and a view of the whole valley."

"You were here with the Bastards before," Stevie says. He's never forgotten this fierce girl.

"I was their captive, like Tarek. Thank you for taking me in."

Both Amy and Tarek smell of smoke and dirt.

"Come sit down. You must be hungry?" Vega offers.

"We're good. We brought food and water." Amy sits down on a chair at the table.

"How did you escape from the Bastards?" Stevie asks.

Tarek grimaces and Amy grins. "I disabled them with a pretty white trumpet flower."

"Those are highly poisonous and hallucinogenic!" Vega sounds alarmed.

"I think most of them will survive."

Stevie is impressed by Amy's cold-blooded courage, but he's still not sure about this girl.

"Most of them?" Greg groans. He seems to be more horrified than impressed.

"And then we crossed paths with a mountain lion," Tarek says.

"Tarek chased him off," Amy says with a grateful look in Tarek's direction.

"A mountain lion?" Stevie says. "How big?"

"It was bigger than a man and all muscle." Tarek sounds relieved and a bit proud of himself.

Before Stevie can ask any more questions, Eleni runs into the room and throws herself at Tarek. Rose wakes up as well and staggers in sleepily to embrace Tarek with tears in her eyes.

Vega brings two large glasses of cold water. "Have something to drink. You've been through quite an ordeal."

"You have a well?" Amy takes a sip of water and smiles approvingly.

Vega nods.

"Can I take a shower? I've been dreaming about a shower. It's been a very long time." Amy smiles crookedly at Vega.

"Of course. I'll give you some fresh clothes."

Amy beams and the two women leave in the direction of the bathroom.

"How did you get out of there?" Rose is sitting next to Tarek, her arms around him, while Eleni bounces on his knees.

"With Amy's help. She freed me. But we need to get ready. The Bastards will be here soon, and they'll be furious. She killed the dogs, and probably Johnny and set the Old Theatre on fire."

"At least you're safe, and you're here. We had no idea how to rescue you, and they threatened to ..." Greg stops and swallows.

"I'm glad you didn't give in to their demands. You can't trust these guys. They would have killed me anyway."

Amy returns, wearing one of Vega's dresses. A green one cut low in the neck. It's a bit too tight on Amy, but brings out her figure. Her skin is glowing.

"Wow." Stevie says a little too quickly and immediately feels like an idiot.

"It feels so good to be clean. Tarek, you want to go next?"

Tarek nods, gives Eleni a big hug, and goes to find some clean clothes. Amy steps closer to the glass doors and looks out over the valley. A smudge of light appears at the horizon. "It's almost dawn."

"We have to find you a place to sleep." Vega busies herself with towels and bed sheets.

"There is no time for sleep," Amy says. "We have to get ready. Let's go over the strategy. They'll probably wake up around noon."

"If we have to fight, I need a few more hours of sleep." Greg goes back into their bedroom and Vega follows.

Amy turns to Stevie. "I need to see the layout of this place."

"I'll show you around. Come on," Stevie offers.

They slip out the door and walk up the dirt road. Amy turns toward Kosmik Peak.

"They're not going to come from up there." Stevie says. "It's a dead end. They'll be coming down this dirt road. We have a motion detector right over there." Stevie looks at Amy. Suspicion lurks in the back of his mind. Why would she want to go up Kosmik Peak?

"I need to go up there, for an overview."

"I don't think you're going to see much, except maybe the cabin."

"Yes, that's it."

Side by side they climb the steep trail. In the pre-dawn gray, the cabin below is just a blur. Stevie involuntarily stops at the place where they found Jack's body.

"Is this where you found him?" Amy asks and kneels down.

"What are you talking about?" Alarm bells go off in Stevie's mind. His heart rate accelerates.

"Jack. Is this where he lay?" She fingers a bunch of purple flowers in the middle of the path. "Purple Penstemon," she murmurs. "I know what that means."

"What did you say? Are these more poisonous flowers?" Stevie is confused. What does she know about the dead man?

"No, the opposite. Penstemon flowers have healing powers. The native tribes used their roots against chest and stomach pain, and a concoction of their leaves against chills and fevers."

"How do you know that?" Stevie picks one of the flowers and hands it to Amy.

She takes it and smiles, nodding. "My mom taught me about plants. So, this is where you found Jack?" She points at the spot on the ground.

"What do you mean? You're creeping me out, Amy!"

"It's okay, Stevie, you can tell me. We are on the same side now."

"What did Tarek tell you?"

"Who are the early risers in your family?"

"My Dad and Lin sometimes. Why are you asking?"

"Okay. We can go back now. Let's go look at your defensive strategy for the house."

"But don't you want to see where the attackers are coming from?"

"It's not necessary. I got the picture. But thanks, you helped me a lot."

He walks behind her down the path, confused, concerned and intrigued. He can't help noticing her legs and bottom muscles flexing under the clinging green dress. She places her steps with confidence and determination in her black army boots, which somehow manage to look sexy with the dress.

BY THE TIME they get back, everybody is up at the cabin. They inspect the new girl and give Tarek hugs of relief. Rose is crying with gratitude and won't let go of his hand. Eleni is sitting on his lap and refuses to budge. Midnight camps at their feet. Lin is giving Amy a pair of black jeans and a long-sleeve T-shirt. Much better battle attire than the green clingy dress. Vega makes coffee.

Stevie tries to get everybody's attention. He's the general in the room.

"People, we have to get ready for battle. The attack is imminent. The Bastards can be here any moment. Let's go over the plan." He unrolls a large map of the property on which he outlined the battle strategy. Everybody moves closer.

"I devised this strategy based on *The Art of War* by Sun Tzu. It uses the elements of deception, terrain, and unity, momentum, fluidity, and turning weaknesses into strength."

"Okay, Stevie, get to the point. We don't have all day," Greg interrupts.

"We have one more asset at our disposal, which is intelligence. We have Amy, who knows the Bastards much better than they know us. Sun Tzu says, 'If you know the enemy and know yourself, you need not fear.' So, Amy, what strategy do you expect the Superior Bastards will apply?"

Amy laughs. "None. I've seen them attack, and I've seen them fight. They'll be furious, jump into their vehicle and storm over here weapons drawn without thought or preparation. They don't think ahead. They rely on brute force."

"Good. That'll work perfectly into my battle plan. Do the Superior Bastards have a leader?"

"Yes, Hermann, the guy with the black beard. They're all afraid of him. He's the most violent of them all. He'll be livid when he finds out his dog Goering is dead. Plus, I stabbed him," Amy says with a grin.

"If we can take out their leader, half the battle is won," Stevie says.

"What should we do?" Hilde asks.

"Right, Hilde, Inge and Eleni, you go to the dugout. Take Midnight with you, and hide with the supplies. No matter what happens, don't come out or reveal your location."

They nod and get up to leave, gathering more supplies and blankets.

"Second, we need a car. One car has to be sacrificed as a roadblock. Any volunteers?"

Rose raises her hand. "You can use mine. It's old and I don't need it."

A murmur of surprised appreciation runs through the group. But it's not like the car runs anymore after the solar storm.

"Thanks, Aunt Rose."

"We'll place it here at the crest of the road." Stevie points at the map. "Gasoline-soaked rags stuffed into the gas tank can be ignited by a line of gas as soon as the Bastards approach. Tarek and Daniel, you'll throw nails and tacks over the road leading to Rose's car. That will puncture their tires so they have to continue on foot. I predict the Bastards will veer right to lower terrain, where we can pick them off with guns, arrows and projectiles from the garage window and the main house. Lin and

Amy, you're going to stud the slope with as many traps, and holes to break their stride as possible."

"Wait, Stevie. If they just go up the left side of the hill, then they're in and we're vulnerable." Greg says.

"True, that's why one sniper has to be stationed on the hill. A dangerous position, but crucial. This person will also have to light the fuse to set the car on fire. Anybody interested?"

"I'll do it," Amy volunteers. "I'm responsible for setting the Bastards on you. They want revenge for what I did to them. I should be the first position of defense."

"Are you sure?" Stevie wants to give her a way out, because this is the riskiest position and he still has some doubts about her loyalties.

"I'm sure. The Bastards burned my home. This is personal for me. I'd consider it fair justice to set their vehicle on fire."

"Actually, you're setting Rose's vehicle on fire," Stevie corrects her.

"Amy, you don't have to do this," Tarek says. "You're a guest here. It should be someone from the family."

Stevie hears an undertone of hesitation and resistance in Tarek's voice. Either he is afraid for Amy, or he doesn't trust her either.

"I have to do it." Amy sets her shoulders straight and raises her chin defiantly.

Greg decides the matter. "Enough of the banter and

the niceties. We don't have time for that. Okay Amy, you get the hillside position."

"What if we start a forest fire with the car explosion?" Vega asks with a skeptical expression.

Everybody turns to Stevie with looks of concern.

"It's a valid point, Stevie," Greg says.

"I thought of that. We soak the brush on both sides with water, and we need water buckets ready to extinguish any flames that may occur." Stevie feels a surge of adrenaline. It's happening. "Rose and Vega can soak the ground and fill the buckets. The main strategy is to force the attacker onto lower ground, where they will be vulnerable to snipers from the garage, the cabin, and the basement, where Lin and Daniel will hold position, Daniel with arrows, and Lin with arrows and the katana."

"The Bastards outnumber us and have a lot more weapons." Amy looks at the assembled group.

"It won't be easy, I know, but Sun Tzu says, 'He will win who knows how to handle both superior and inferior forces.'"

Daniel rolls his eyes, but Stevie continues unperturbed.

"During the battle, Rose and Vega will throw rocks from the deck."

"Are you kidding me?" Rose cries. "Throw rocks at armed men? That's insane."

"Stevie, is that really necessary?" Greg asks.

Stevie keeps his eyes on the map to make sure he hasn't forgotten anything. "The rocks will distract the Bastards and create stumbling blocks on the steep slope so the snipers can take them out. I'll take position in the garage with one gun, and Greg at the upper cabin window with his Glock. Got it?"

Amy looks at Greg. "You're the ex-cop?"

He nods.

"You can probably use these." Amy opens her backpack and takes out three handguns. Lays them out on the table. "They are .45. cal ACPs."

Stevie beams, totally smitten. All doubts and misgivings about Amy's loyalties are forgotten. If she hands over these handguns used by Navy SEALs, she must be on their side.

"Fantastic! Now we have guns for six snipers. Now Daniel and Lin, plus Tarek can be armed. If I remember right, ACPs can shoot accurately up to fifty meters, or a hundred and fifty feet."

Amy nods. She pulls some boxes out of the backpack. "Here are six boxes of ammunition. That's all I could get."

Tarek looks at Amy with surprise.

Amy wasn't armed during the stand-off with the Bastards, Stevie remembers. But she seems to know a lot about handguns.

"Do the Bastards have rifles?"

Both Tarek and Amy nod.

"But we have the higher ground, literally," Stevie

continues. "Greg will go over how to use the Sigs with Daniel, Lin, myself, and Tarek. Any questions?"

People shake their heads no.

"Let's go and prepare, or as Sun Tzu says, 'He will win who prepared himself, waits to take the enemy unprepared.'"

"Give it rest with your Sun Tzu quotes," Daniel grumbles.

22

DAY 53: 3 HOURS LATER: STEVIE

The terrain is prepared. They pushed Rose's Camry up the hill to block the access road. The stretch of road before the car is studded with nails. Full water buckets are ready on the hillside. All have changed into leather jackets, boots, gloves and beanies. Amy is wearing a pair of Lin's black jeans (they are a bit tight on her), combat boots, and a camouflage jacket. She hid her hair under a brown beanie and smudged her face with charcoal from the end of a burned cork. Stevie thinks she looks fiercely amazing. Her eyes burn intensely in her darkened face. He's worried about her safety and her loyalty but, of course, he hides his feelings. As always, Lin looks neat and ready, her hair in a tight top knot.

They've eaten a light meal. Now they wait. This is the hard part. Stevie thinks of the Game of Thrones episode about the night before the epic battle at Winterfell. They're ready for the Nightwalkers. But what to do until it begins? In the GOT episode, everybody sat around the fire the night before the battle contemplating mortality. He doesn't want to go there. That's Vega's territory. She and Rose look glum. He needs to do something to lift the moral. A speech before the battle? He looks at his dad. Greg's oiling and reassembling his Glock. Amy stares defiantly out the window, and Tarek looks stricken. These two know what the Bastards are capable of. They have seen them in action first hand.

Fortunately, Inge, Eleni, Midnight, and Hilde are in the dugout. Stevie prays they will be safe. Stevie is racking his brain about how to rally his troops. He clears his throat. Everybody looks at him.

That's when the red light blinks and the fire alarm goes off.

Stevie doesn't have to say anything, or yell "battle stations." Everybody knows what to do and where to go. Silently, they move to their stations. Amy slinks out the door, across the driveway and into the shrubs of the hillside above the road block of Rose's car. Stevie's takes his place across the dirt road from her, in the garage. He will cover the first wave of attack from the windows, as the Bastards maneuver around the roadblock.

He hears cursing and yelling from the crest of the road as the Bastards' tires are punctured. Good. The nails worked. Now they have to advance on foot.

As planned, fourteen Bastards come over the hill down towards Rose's car, weapons drawn, yelling, "You motherfuckers. We'll show you," and shooting into the air. Good, wasting their ammunition. *Please, Amy, light the fuse!*

They get closer and Stevie hears crackling as the gasoline line ignites and runs toward the car. *Will it explode? Are the gas-soaked rags going to work?*

The fire line stops short of the car. What interrupted its flow? Stevie's heart lurches as Amy jumps out of the shrubs and tries to reignite it with her lighter. She's too close to the explosion!

"There she is, that bitch," Blackbeard yells. "You're going to pay for killing Goering and Johnny!"

Amy reignites the fire line again, and tries to retreat back into the bushes. But she's too late. The explosion fills the air with a deafening boom, and rocks fly in all directions. Just as the car goes up in flames, Stevie sees the advancing leader of the Bastards thrown back by the shockwave. Where is Amy?

Stevie's about to run out and look for Amy, when she emerges out of the smoke. Blackbeard scrambles up from the ground and is at her throat.

Stevie can't shoot him without hitting Amy. The Bastard has her by the neck. *Oh. My. God.* He feels lightheaded as if all blood had drained out of his brain. He can't afford to faint. He must push through. He forces himself to take a deep breath, pushing air into his lungs.

Amy coughs. "Goering deserved it, and so do you! You burned our house, my mother ..."

Blackbeard chokes her harder. "We let your mother go in exchange for you. That was the deal. You broke it."

Amy gasps for air.

Tarek runs out of the house, where he was supposed to cover the entrance, his gun drawn. "Leave her alone!" he yells. He barrels up the driveway toward Amy and Blackbeard.

Tarek's deserted his post. Adrenaline kicks in, and suddenly Stevie feels like he has too much blood in his head. It's about to explode.

"Tarek, no, go back!" Amy croaks.

Blackbeard turns, aims and fires. Tarek goes down. But his movement gives Stevie a clear line of fire. He aims, squeezes the trigger. Blackbeard goes down.

A mini-second of relief.

A collective groan goes up from the remaining Bastards as their leader falls. Amy scrambles toward Tarek.

What to do? Stevie wonders if he should help them. What was that about Amy's mother?

Stevie needs to refocus. He turns toward the advancing Bastards, who are coming around the car. As expected, they're running downhill alongside the garage. Greg is firing from the upstairs window of the cabin, but Stevie's closer. Rose runs out of the house to Tarek. She and Amy drag him inside.

Okay, he needs to concentrate. He aims, shoots. Hits one of the Bastards. He's going down. Others stumble and fall, groaning, as they step into the traps. Nice. No time to think, just react. Aim, shoot another. Like a video game.

One of the Bastards looks up, sees Vega throwing rocks from the deck and aims. Vega screams and the shooter grins. Stevie fires. The shooter drops. But what about his mom? Stevie hopes Amy and Rose will pull Vega inside.

"Vega!" his dad shouts. Is he leaving his post to help her?

"Dad," Stevie screams, "stay at your post." He can't believe his dad would put Vega above the fight. Too much is at stake here.

Daniel gets one Bastard from the basement window with his Sig Sauer. As they round to the north side of the house, Lin pops another. Nine more to go.

Stevie moves to another window in the garage overlooking the northern hillside where the Bastards have advanced.

He sees Midnight racing out from the dugout, barking, trying to defend his territory. Oh, no, Eleni is running after him. "Midnight!" she screams.

The Bastards on the hillside turn toward the dog and the girl. *Why couldn't they stay put?* Inge runs after Eleni. "Go back, Eleni! Now! Let Midnight go!" Inge yells. Eleni stops. Looks uncertain. Inge reaches her. Two shots ring out. Inge throws herself in front of Eleni, who turns and races back to the hideout. Inge falls. Midnight escapes into the forest.

Stevie gets the shooter. But Grandma Inge is down. He groans. How can he get to her?

They're outnumbered. They're outgunned. Three of his people are down. The attackers have advanced beyond his range. In a few moments, they'll reach Daniel and Lin in the basement. His Dad has left his post. Lin is still shooting, but she can't see beyond the slope. Stevie feels a hard pit in his stomach. What would Sun Tzu do?

He grits his teeth and keeps shooting, but there are too many attackers. Tears run down his face. The Bastards keep advancing, stumbling over the lifeless form of Grandma Inge. Stevie shoots until he runs out of ammunition. He hears no more shots from Daniel or Lin below him, and none from his dad above him in the cabin. They must be out of ammunition as well.

It's over. Below, Daniel and Lin come out of the basement with raised arms in surrender.

Surrender? It's the only way to keep them from reaching the dugout and slaughtering Eleni and Hilde. Will they spare the rest of them? There's no guarantee. He makes the decision. He wants to continue the fight, in hand-to-hand combat with the katanas. But what good are Japanese swords against firearms? All this races through his head at lightning speed. Now all that matters is to save lives, Daniel, Lin, his dad, his mom, Tarek, Rose, the people in the dugout, Amy ... Fuck Sun Tzu. He grabs a white drop cloth from a pile in the garage. Waves it out the window. "We surrender!" he shouts.

A FEW BASTARDS LOOK UP. They take aim and shoot at the pillowcase. Laugh. Stevie quickly pulls back his hand. They have no leader. Who's going to make the decisions now? Greg steps out on the balcony waving a large white bed sheet. "Cease fire. We want to discuss terms of surrender. Who is your leader?"

Laughter from below. Daniel and Lin are on their knees, hands in the air. Shots in the air, some hit the bed sheet, some ricochet off the metal barrier around the deck. "You killed our leader!" they shout.

Stevie watches helplessly, cringing at the utter defeat. Sees his grandma's body on the slope. Wonders if his mother is still alive? Feels something rip inside.

"What do you want?" he shouts out the window.

"We want everything! Your house, land, and supplies." A man with a red beard steps forward. Their new leader?

Stevie bristles with resistance.

Greg walks out on the deck, stands up tall, above the metal barrier. Opens his arms wide. He's unarmed. There's no more ammunition. "Let us go, and you can have the premises."

Stevie feels all the air go out of his chest. He deflates. Utter defeat.

Redbeard pauses. Looks around at the seven companions he has left. They stand behind him, weapons drawn, aiming at Greg. Waiting for his signal. He turns around.

"Go. Now. Before I change my mind. All the provisions stay."

Stevie crumbles on the floor, but his father has done the only reasonable thing. He saved their lives. Stevie's mind races. With any luck, the Bastards don't know about the dugout. The supplies there.

"We have a critically wounded woman here. We need to carry her out," Greg says calmly, arms still spread wide.

So, Stevie's mom is alive.

"Anything else? You have to go to the bathroom first or take a shower?" Redbeard mocks. "Out, now!" He takes aim at Greg, fires, and barely misses.

Greg ducks back into the house.

Stevie runs out of the garage and into the main house, where he finds Greg, Rose, Tarek and Amy, huddled around Vega on the ground. She's bleeding heavily.

VEGA:

The fog has come in and she can only see blurry outlines. Faces appear and recede in the mist. Greg's voice reaches her from far away.

"... go to dugout ... detour ... whatever you can grab..."

Stevie's face swims into view. "Mom." He says as if from far away.

"Stevie ... it will be fine ..."

She tries to reach out, but can't lift her arm, can't breathe very well, something blocks the air from flowing into her lungs.

She floats off into an empty space. It's dark, but a tiny glow in the distance pulls her like a magnet. It looks nice, welcoming. She wants to go there. She floats in the direction of the light and leaves her body on the floor behind. The light expands and brightens.

She encounters snatches from her life. Greg and her, running down a street in the rain, laughing. They both look so young. Driving with Greg through Tuscany on a Vespa on a hot summer's day, and finding a waterfall by chance. Swimming in the cool pool of water. Looking into Daniel's face for the first time after giving birth, recognizing each other; Daniel's first step—trying to reach her and his purple whale. Stevie with a butterfly on his head. Holding her first published book in her hands. Seeing a Vermeer painting for the first time at the Rijksmuseum in Amsterdam. Waking up on Christmas Day their first year at the cabin, when they still slept on mats on the floor, and finding the whole property covered by a pristine blanket of snow, waiting for their first footsteps. Having a dance party on the deck of the cabin at night under the stars and a string of lights, dancing to Van Morrison's Moondance song with Stevie. Hiking up Volcan Mountain with her family on a cold winter's day and seeing the desert and the ocean from the top. Walking up Kosmik Peak and seeing the sun set in a dip of El Cajon Mountain on the Winter Solstice. Seeing a Golden Eagle soar over the lake.

A sharp pain in her chest and abdomen sucks her back into her body. She moans.

Greg's face emerges from the fog. There are dark circles under his eyes and a smear of dirt on his cheek. Red splatters on his forehead and chin make her wince. She tries to smile at him.

"We have to move you to the dugout," he says.

Something soft is pushed under her head. It hurts. She wants to go back to the light.

"Hang on, Vega. Please, for me ..." Greg pleads. "She needs a doctor."

He sounds desperate, worried. Vega wants to tell him everything's fine, but she can't make her mouth form the words. And she's so tired. Why can't they let her sleep? Vaguely she sees a figure, with a bandage around his arm. She hears voices, but she doesn't know what are they talking about. It couldn't be her. She closes her eyes, hoping to find the light again.

STEVIE:

Stevie looks around the cabin's living room, eyes wild with terror and panic. His mother is losing consciousness. Tarek has a bloody bandage on his arm. Stevie can't process what happened, he can't take it all in. Amy sees his confusion.

"Snap out of it, Steven! Get supplies, whatever you can grab!" Amy looks at his father. "Greg, it's bad. The bullet is still lodged in Vega's side. I don't like the sound of her breathing."

"She needs a hospital," Greg interrupts. "Vega, can you hear me?"

"Here's some antibiotic salve from the first aid kit." Tarek holds out a tube to Greg.

"Thanks, but that's not enough. She needs ..." Greg says.

"She needs ... my mother," Amy finishes.

"What?"

"My mother is a healer. She can treat Vega. The hospital is not an option. It's too far, if it's even functioning ..."

"Where is your mother?" Stevie asks.

"I think I can find her. Take Vega to the dugout. Try to stop the bleeding. I'll take Steven with me."

Tarek takes one end of the blanket with a grimace. His arm obviously hurts.

Amy gently puts her hand his arm. "Tarek, thank you for saving my life. Blackbeard almost got me."

Tarek tries to smile. It comes out crooked.

Amy turns back to Greg. "Stay with her, don't let her drift off. We'll be as quick as possible."

Greg nods and cradles Vega's head on the pillow.

"We have to go now. They're furious, especially with you, Amy," Stevie says.

Amy pauses. "We'll slip out the back way and go up the hill. The Bastards are so busy celebrating they won't notice we've left."

BEFORE HE KNOWS IT, Stevie is putting one foot in front of the other on the path leading up to Kosmik Peak.

This is the worst day of my life! Stevie scrambles after Amy. He's dazed. Tears stream down his face. *I was supposed to win this battle, lead the troops, save our home.*

He doesn't blame the defeat on anyone but himself. They all did what they could and more. Grandma Inge threw herself into the path of a bullet. Amy fought like a tiger. His mom threw stones at armed militiamen—as he had told her—and got shot, maybe fatally.

Now they have to leave with no place to go. He should have let his dad take charge. Maybe he would have been a better leader.

He stumbles over a large rock in the path. Looking back, he sees the black spots that give the leopard rocks their name. Amy's fiercely marching ahead, ignoring him.

"Why do I have to come with you? I just went through an intense battle, my grandma died, my mom is critically injured. I'm exhausted. I'm traumatized."

Amy stops and turns around. "Steven, you have to

calm down and you have to grow up. Stop whining. You're helping nobody by spinning out of control. Not your mother, not your grandmother, not yourself."

"I just wasn't prepared for people dying, getting seriously hurt. It's painful. I feel responsible. And why are you calling me Steven?"

"Stevie is a child's name, and you're a man now. If you want to play war, you have to be able to deal with the losses. And you did save my life. So, thank you for that."

"You're welcome. I'm just glad you got away from Blackbeard? But ..."

"No buts. We have to find my mother fast." Amy begins climbing again.

Steven swallows. "I killed five people ..."

"The battle is over. Now we need to save your mother."

Steven sighs and trudges after her. He tries to figure out how many hours it's been since he slept. His breathing is short and shallow. His thoughts flit all over the place. The moment of surrender. The casualties.

Steven forms a circle with his mouth and breathes out very slowly. Four counts in, and six counts out through the nose. He begins to feel calmer. His Mom taught him this breathing exercise. The surroundings come back into focus. Amy has stopped at the spot where Greg found Jack's body.

"Why are you stopping?" he asks.

"This is where you found Jack," Amy says.

"How do you ...?"

"The purple penstemons. I saw them the first time we came up here."

"What do the flowers have to do with anything?"

"They're a message from my mother. You have to help me find the next patch of penstemon, Steven."

"I've seen them ..." Steven looks around, trying to remember.

"Okay, take me there."

Steven grabs Amy's hand and pulls her up to the summit of Kosmik Peak, then behind the viewing platform. He points to a clump of purple flowers with bell-shaped blossoms. "I saw them here when we were looking for Tarek. What do you call them? *Pestemon?*"

"Penstemon flowers. They are native to this area. The Cahuilla Indians called them 'hummingbird's kiss' and used them for skin rashes and irritation. My mother planted this clump as a message, so I could find her. She knew I'd understand." Amy bends down and inspects the ground for other signs from her mother.

"Amy, There's a deer path right behind the flowers!"

"Nice, Steven. That's why I brought you along."

"What do these flowers have to do with your mother and Jack?"

Amy sighs. "I'll explain later. Let's follow this trail. We don't have much time."

Steven nods. The image of his mother trying to raise her arm, trying to comfort him, punches him in the stomach. He's been so critical and impatient with her. He

assumed there'd always be time to make up with her. Now
she teeters between life and death. "Let's go faster."

Tall grasses and ceanothus brush scratch his legs. It's
easy to lose the trail. Amy goes first, pausing occasionally
to find the narrow, overgrown trail. She stops abruptly.
Holds her finger to her lips.

Steven listens closely. He hears the rattling. "Rat-
tlesnake," he whispers.

She nods.

Steven starts to shiver. Then the adrenaline kicks in.
He remembers his survival book. "Freeze and back off
slowly," Steven says quietly.

Amy backs off ever so slowly. Steven still hears the
high frequency rattle. He retreats as well. Is the rattling
sound coming closer or fading away? He's grateful they're
both wearing hi-top boots.

"I can't hear it anymore," Steven says.

"Me neither."

"Okay, follow me." Steven picks up a stick and beats
the grass it in front of him on the ground. "Stay close."

They creep forward along the trail. With each tentative step, Steven thinks of his mother. He can't let her
down. She's always been there for him. He remembers
when he was little and afraid of a ghost in his closet at
night. His mom made up a ritual of putting a little Buddha
figure on a shelf with the sweaters. That took care of his
fear and he slept well from then on.

Steven feels like they've been hiking for hours. He has

lost all sense of time. He drinks from his water bottle. But his mind is only half there.

The brush thins as they enter a dense patch of sugar pines and live oak trees.

"Steven, look!" Amy points ahead at a small shack listing dangerously to the left.

"That's an old, abandoned homestead from the gold rush days."

"Maybe that's where my mother is."

They break into a run. But the shack is empty. A rotting front door hanging on one hinge, creaking floorboards threaten to break under their steps. An old wicker chair with a broken seat stands alone in a corner.

"Let's go. This place isn't safe." Steven takes Amy's arm and tries to pull her outside.

Amy gives him a desolate look of defeat.

VEGA:

Greg's face floats above her in a disembodied way. Why does he look so blurry?

"Vega?" he says. She sees his mouth move and then hears words, but the two things don't seem to be connected. She tries to tell him she's okay, not to worry, not to speak, but a sharp pain shoots through her arm, down her spine making her moan.

"Stay with me, Vega, help is coming. But we need to move you."

She no longer has the oxygen to answer. Raspy noises come out of her mouth, as she tries to pull in more air. She breathes through her nostrils. The air does not reach deep enough to give relief. If she slowed down her breathing, maybe she could last on the oxygen left in her lungs.

She hears a crack and sharp, cool air rushes in. She sucks it in, but the cold air burns like fire in her chest. She hears Daniel's voice

"Dad, we have to leave now. What should we do with grandma's body?"

"The living come first. We can't leave your mom," Greg's says.

Daniel comes into view, but he's also so damn white and the outlines of his face oscillate. Vega gasps for air.

"Oh, my God. Mom, can you hear me?

She nods as best as she can. Tries to focus on Daniel's voice, but he sounds distorted, like a long draw out moan —"*Moooummm ...*" Is he speaking to her?

Her pulse drowns out every other sound. The edges of her vision pull back. The world darkens. She licks her dried lips with her tongue.

"Waateeer ..." she hears from far away. Feels cool liquid touch her lips.

"Daaaaniel stayyyy withhh heeer," Greg's voice drawls. She tries to nod again. Feels a hand touch hers. Daniel's head bends over her hand. She feels warm tears on her skin. She tries to shake her head. Don't cry. But her pulse is deafening. Her inhalations get shallower. She feels the blood in her ears. Feels the blood in her stomach. A door opens, and the rush of cool air washes over her again.

A sharp voice shouts, "Get going, now, and leave the food!"

A shot rings out, lodges in the wall above Vega's head. She flinches.

Vega feels her body being lifted at both ends, sagging in the middle. A sharp razor pain shoots through her side. A weight drops hard on her chest. She can't breathe. She is drowning. Pulling air in through her nose, she concentrates on benign knowledge. Her glance falls on the Tibetan Thangka of the goddess Tara on the wall, her kind smile, her hands open in a gift bestowing gesture. How auspicious that she brought it from home when they found out about the solar storm. Tara, full of compassion, ready to step down from her lotus throne to help those in need. Vega needs her now. Tara's mantra *Om Tare tu tare tu res vaha,* emerges from somewhere in Vega's mind. She feels Tara's presence. She is not afraid.

GREG:

Greg and Daniel carry Vega's blanket. Tarek, Rose, and Lin follow behind, carrying sleeping bags and water. They form a pathetic procession. Greg looks back at the cabin. So many hours, so much care and love and resources went into building this refuge. Will he ever see it again? He shakes himself out of the nostalgia impatiently. He needs to deal with the now.

"We'll have to get my mother's body tonight," Greg says to Daniel and points toward the slope. "We can't leave her here."

"Hey faster, down there!" Redbeard mocks and sends a bullet in their direction.

Greg notices he's drinking out of a bottle of Silver Oak from Alexander Valley. A very special vintage he and Vega bought in Sonoma country. Good, Greg thinks. *As long as the wine last, they probably won't follow us.*

Balancing their load, they walk down the slope, side-stepping the bodies of fallen Bastards. Some of the Bastards are raiding Greg's wine cellar in the basement. He hears celebratory laughter, breaking glass, hollering.

He's grateful Amy and Steven are out of danger.

Greg leads his small group of survivors in a detour, in case the Bastards are watching. Fortunately, they seem preoccupied with the spoils of their victory. When Greg reaches a level spot, he decides this is the spot where they are going to bury his mother, Inge. But first they have to take Vega to the dugout.

GREG'S HEART beats as loud as a jackhammer in his chest. They can't make any noise, can't give themselves away. But trudging through the underbrush with five people, including one unconscious woman in a blanket stretcher, is loud.

Under cover of the live oak trees, he swings northwest, circling back to the dugout. The laughing and hollering from the cabin, drown out their movements. The Bastards are too drunk to track them.

As they approache the small clearing with the dugout, it's eerily quiet. He can't hear anything. Are Eleni and Hilde gone? Did the Bastards find them? Did they run away in fear? His heart skips a beat.

He pushes aside the hanging branches covering the entrance like a curtain. Eleni and Hilde are cowering in a corner.

"Relax, it's me!" he says and steps inside. The dugout roof is so low, he has to stoop.

"Thank God, it's you," Hilde answers with a big sigh. "Is it over?"

Greg nods. Eleni rushes out into Tarek's arms. "Daddy, you're hurt!" She fingers the bandage on this arm.

"Nothing bad; it will heal quickly." He cradles her head and inhales the scent of her hair.

"Well, good, so we can go back to the cabin now." Hilde gets up from her camping chair, pulling down her blue woolen sweater.

"No, Hilde," Greg stammers, "W-we lost."

"What do you mean?" Hilde raises her eyebrows.

"We lost the cabin, Hilde. I'm just here to bring Vega.

She's badly hurt. You two stay put. And I need to get a pickax and a shovel to bury Inge."

Greg carefully moves inside and beds Vega down on a mat in the dugout. Daniel helps him lift her off the blanket. She is unconscious, but her cheek burns red with fever. Greg pushes Vega's hair, wet with sweat, out of her face.

"I'll get help," he whispers. "You just hang on."

He turns around and crawls out of the dugout, where Hilde confronts him. "Inge?"

"Inge didn't make it," Greg hangs his head.

"Oh, no, my friend Inge!" Hilde wails. "I must say good-bye to her."

"No Hilde, you can't leave. These are all the supplies we have now. This is everything we have left. We can't allow the Bastards to find this dugout."

"What about the others?"

"Amy and Steven went to find Amy's mother, because Vega is badly hurt. Everyone else is here. I'll take Daniel with me and we'll be back as soon as we have buried Inge."

"But there's no space here."

"I know." Greg crouches down and finds the shovel and pickax they used to dig this shelter.

Hilde takes a deep breath, straightens her spine and composes herself. "Very well, we'll find a way. Here, I want you to take this, for Inge. I want her to have it. It's from Germany." She takes a small pin—a good luck charm—in the shape of a four-leaf clover covered with garnets off her sweater and hands it to Greg.

"Are you sure?" he asks.

"I'm sure. I don't need it. I don't believe in good luck anymore. Go now, and get back quickly."

Greg pockets the pin and grabs the shovel and pickax.

"Take this for mom." Rose stops him and hands him a small golden crucifix on a thin chain. Greg accepts it. He didn't know his sister was religious, but in a situation like this any bit of comfort helps.

"Tarek, you guard the dugout. Here's my Glock with three bullets."

Tarek nods and takes the weapon. Greg and Daniel disappear quietly out of the opening and into the forest.

23

DAY 53: 6 HOURS LATER: GREG

Back at the hillside Greg waits with Daniel for darkness. He doesn't want the Bastards to know where they are, and he wants to retrieve his mother's body.

The sun sets in ridiculous glory. How can it glow so beautifully on such a cruel day?

In the twilight, Greg steals back to the slope to get Inge's body. He's never been a soldier, never been to war, but the scene before him reminds him of the urban battlefield he's seen as a police man. Nine bodies sprawl across the field at unnatural, lifeless angles. It takes Greg a minute to refocus on the task at hand. It seems obscene to bury one body and leave the rest exposed, but they are not his responsibility. He locates his mother. Her pale face and the bloody hole in her chest, break his spirit. Too much loss in one day; his mother, his home, maybe even Vega. He bends and spreads the white bed sheet he brought over the lifeless body, sobbing.

A drunken scream from the wine cellar shakes Greg back from grief into functioning mode, going on emergency autopilot. He recalls his training. There are always casualties in urban warfare. He needs to bury Inge with as much respect as possible in the current situation. He wraps her into the sheet and hefts the small body over his shoulder, stumbling back to the spot where Daniel is waiting.

AN OWL SWOOPS from the left and glides over the field in front of the slope. The raptor catches an updraft and soars into the sky towards North Peak in the last fading light of the day. For a moment Greg sees the scene from the owl's perspective, birds' eye view. In the moonlight, a stubbly grass clearing gives way to Manzanita bushes and oak trees further down in the valley. The view encompasses the whole Shelter Valley, Vulcan and Palomar Mountains, backed by a glimpse of the snowy peaks of San Jacinto Range in the far distance. It's a good place to bury his mother. If it weren't for the drunken laughter coming from the cabin, it would be peaceful.

Greg takes the shovel and gives the ax to Daniel. The Bastards aren't watching, content with their victory, the cabin, the supplies. Amy was right, 'They don't have much of a plan."

Daniel and Greg dig. The ground is hard.

"This reminds me when we were digging the hideout," Daniel says.

"Thank God we did. But this time we're digging a grave."

The grave is not very deep and not very big, just big enough for Inge's body. They lay her shrouded figure in carefully. Greg remembers Hilde's pin and attaches it to the bed sheet. Daniel has found some wild sage. He throws it into the grave. "They're supposed to keep away evil spirits," he mumbles. Then Greg and Daniel fill in the hole with dirt, while Daniel fashions a small cross out of two oak branches.

"Her long journey has come to an end. She came from Germany to New York to Palm Springs to this mountain. She leaves behind a daughter, a son, and two grandsons. Not a bad legacy." Greg says, as he sticks the cross into the ground.

"And thanks to her, Eleni is still alive," Daniel adds with bowed head.

Greg puts his hand on Daniel's shoulder. "It's been a long day." Greg leans on the shovel. "We need to get back to the dugout."

"Good-bye, grandma," Daniel mumbles, and carries the pickax on his shoulder.

. . .

STEVEN:

Amy kneels on the ground in the gold rush shack. The old floorboards are surprisingly clean, as if someone had swept them. In a corner, Amy finds a bundle of dried wild sage, singed by fire. She touches the plants, rubs their silvery leaves, smells her fingers. "This is recent. Smell this." She holds the bundle up for Steven.

He smells the pungent, earthy herb.

"Burning bundles of sage purifies a space. She was here. My mother must have been here a short while ago."

Steven crouches besides Amy, not sure what to do next. A muffled sound from the entrance makes him freeze. "Someone's here," he whispers, looking for a way out. But there is only one door.

Amy turns around. "Mom."

A woman steps through the low entrance and straightens herself inside. Her curly dark hair is gathered in a messy bun on her head. She's wearing a long, gray, skirt and a woolen wrap. Standing in the shade of the shack, she looks like a figure from the 18th century. Her arms open wide. "Amy!"

Mother and daughter fall into each other's arms, while Steven watches, not wanting to intrude. He feels pressure in his chest, like he's about to cry. He sniffs and clears his throat. There is the matter of his own mother, whom he suddenly misses with a vengeance. Hopefully, they have found Amy's mother in time. Hopefully, Vega won't keep thinking of him as the angry brat he was lately.

"Mom, this is Steven."

Steven realizes the women have approached him and now stand right in front of him.

"Hello Steven, I'm Claire." Amy's mother extends her hand.

Steven takes the hand, which has a strong grasp; he feels callouses. These hands have worked hard.

"Delighted to meet you, but we have to hurry," Steven urges. "We need medicine for my mother, and something to remove a bullet." He presses out the words, gripped by relief that they found Claire and fear that they might be too late.

"I'll have to prepare the medicines." Claire says.

"Thank you," Steven says formally.

"Mom, why did you hide from us?" Amy grasps her mother's hand.

"I wasn't sure who you were at first. Not everything is what it seems on this mountain."

"What do you mean?"

"Jack was murdered not far from here. I had to be careful."

"I saw the spots, the penstemon flowers.'

"Good, Amy. I knew you would get the message."

"Did you see who did it?"

"No, but I watched him die." Claire fingers a bunch of penstemon flowers in her basket. "I couldn't do anything for him anymore, but I was with him and held him. His last word was your name, Amy."

"He said my name?" Amy hangs her head.

Listening to their exchange, the hairs on Steven's arms raise up. Why are they talking about Jack like that?

"He loved you a lot," Claire puts her arm around Amy.

"I know. He protected me from the other Bastards. It got a lot worse after he was gone." Amy's voice is hardly above a whisper.

"Wasn't Jack a member of the Superior Bastards?" Steven asks, his mind reeling.

"He was a good man, in his own way." Claire strokes Amy's back.

"They burned down your home!" Steven protests.

"Without Jack they would have killed me as well." Claire straightens and looks Steven straight into the eye. "What did you do with his body?"

Steven motions toward the edge of the cliff. "Threw him down the ravine."

"He was looking for me, to reunite me with my daughter."

"I don't understand," Steven admits. This day just never ends. It's too much. Tarek coming back with Amy; losing the battle against the Bastards; now this. He sits down on the floor, his head in his hands, exhausted and confused. Amy puts her hand on his back. It feels comforting, but only a little.

"I had to assume it was a member of your family who killed him," Claire continues.

"We are not murderers," Steven declares and remembers the five Bastards he killed today.

"Did he say who killed him?" Amy asks her mother.

"I asked him who did this to him. He was barely conscious. He muttered something like 'high voice.' I asked him, 'Was it a woman?' He may have nodded, but I can't be sure."

Steven hears a ringing in his ears. He feels lightheaded, and the room around him is spinning. Everything he assumed is turned upside down. Jack was a good man, Amy loved him, and now Claire is claiming that a woman killed him. His world is coming apart at the seams.

"The Bastards burnt our house right after the solar storm. We didn't have enough plunder. They were going to kill my mother. Jack intervened. They agreed to let her go, if I came with them. That's how we got separated."

"If it hadn't been for Jack ..." Claire begins.

Steven gets up and tries to pull himself together. "You loved this Jack?" he asks Amy. "After he burned down your house?"

"I felt affection and gratitude. He saved my mother, and he risked his life for me."

Steven shakes his head. His infatuation for Amy is turning into weariness. "This is like me being grateful to the Bastards for sparing my life after they stole our home and killed my grandma."

"I suppose they could have killed you too."

"We're getting our home back." Steven is confident his dad will find a way.

Both women nod and smile indulgently at him.

"Fair enough," Claire says, cutting the conversation short.

"Can we go back to my mother now?" Steven asks. These two really try his patience.

"I need to assemble the right medicines. You two can help me. We have a few hours before it's getting dark. We'll stay here overnight to prepare and then go first thing in the morning."

Steven nods, even though the thought of staying another night makes him nauseous with anxiety. Will they get back in time for his mother? Can he trust Amy and Claire? He has no choice but to grow up and deal with the situation. "What do you need?" he asks.

Claire looks through the bundles of herbs in her basket. "I still have some aloe vera cactus. Their gel is important for wound healing. I have garlic." She pulls out a large string of garlic bulbs. "It's a natural antibiotic and blood thinner. It brings down fever and blood pressure. Turmeric can be used as an anti-inflammatory in tea."

Maybe she does know her stuff, Steven thinks. "What about the bullet?" he asks.

"If it hasn't harmed any organs, it's better to leave it. But I do need calendula. I need your help to find and pick the large orange flowers. I also need its root to make a wound healing paste. And I need honey."

"We have a beehive on the property. We can get a comb and extract the honey without being noticed." Steven says. He had no idea honey had healing properties.

"Fantastic. Propolis is a little wonder ingredient; bees use it to seal their hive. It contains resin and it is anti-bacterial, helps against viruses and fungi, and it's anti-inflammatory and heals skin wounds."

The bees on their property have been working hard to produce medicine for his mom.

"Let's go before it gets dark. I've seen some calendula flowers on the other side of the mountain. Their bloom is almost over, but we only need the dried flowers anyway." Claire gives them small burlap bags and leads them northeast. There is no trail, so Steven has to place his feet carefully, and hope exhaustion won't take over.

Mother and daughter walk in front of him, arm in arm. What are these two women playing at? What do they want from him? No matter, he has to put his personal feelings aside in order to save his mother.

GREG:

Greg and Daniel stumble down to the dugout, barely able to stand. They haven't eaten in sixteen hours, have fought against an overwhelming enemy; lost. They carried Vega up and down this hillside. Dug a grave for his mother, Inge. Daniel collapses outside with Lin and Rose. Greg crawls inside the dugout to check on Vega. Her skin is almost transparent, her eyelids flutter. She looks right through him when he takes her hand, as if she was already somewhere else.

This is too much. This is more than a person can take. Greg squeezes his eyes shut. Where is he going to find the strength to carry on without Vega?

He crawls out of the dugout, finds Lin by Daniel's side. Hilde passes out water bottles from the dugout and distributes the sleeping bags and blankets they brought with them.

GREG FEELS MORE DRAINED and exhausted than he's ever been before. "Vega didn't even recognize me," he says barely audible and collapses in another chair.

They sit in a circle around the propane stove, eating canned minestrone soup Rose heated for them.

"We won't all fit in the dugout," Hilde says, "and it's too cold to sleep out here."

"We can't make a fire. The smoke would be visible from the cabin," Greg says. "Daniel and Tarek, Lin and I will make due with the sleeping bags out here. Hilde, you can sleep inside with Vega, Rose, and Eleni. We just need to eat, re-supply, and rest. Tomorrow Daniel and I will go down to the lake and to find reinforcements to win our cabin back."

Daniel has nodded off in a camping-chair, but he jerks

awake at Greg's statement. "Did you just volunteer me for a recruiting mission to find allies, and another fight with the Bastards tomorrow?" he asks groggily.

"I'll go with you," Lin says quickly to Greg.

"Good, then let's all get some rest."

"What about mom?" Daniel asks.

"Rose and Hilde will have to keep a careful watch on her until Stevie and Amy come back with Amy's mom," Greg says with effort.

Lin scoots closer to Daniel, and he squeezes her hand. "Get some sleep," she whispers. "Tomorrow will be better."

"It can't get much worse than it is," Daniel answers.

"Sure, it could. We could be dead on the hill like Inge, or wounded like Vega," Lin whispers.

24

DAY 54: LIN

At dawn, Greg, Daniel and Lin walk three abreast down Sugar Pine Road. They pass the Bastards' disabled transport vehicle. All tires are punctured. It's quiet below, no sounds from the cabin. As if reading her thoughts, Daniel says, "They're still sleeping it off."

"It wasn't a bad plan," Lin says, trying to keep in step with the two long-legged men.

"It wasn't," Greg admits. "But we were outnumbered and we ran out of ammunition. That's why we need reinforcements." And we need to save Vega, he thinks, still feeling her limp body in the blanket.

Lin slept poorly on the cold ground in front of the dugout, but eventually exhaustion took over. The bread and tea she had for breakfast helped revive her. Thank God for the dugout and its supplies.

She hears rustling in the brush beside them. There is no wind. Something or someone is in there. If it's a mountain lion, they have nothing to defend themselves. Greg left his Glock with the last three bullets at the dugout with Tarek, in case he has to defend the women. But mountain lions are nocturnal creatures, Lin remembers. An animal breaks through the underbrush and runs toward them. They stop in their tracks. It's Midnight.

"Where have you been?" Daniel scratches the black lab behind the ears. The dog wags his tail. "You caused a lot of damage back there, Midnight."

"Yeah," Greg chimes in. "I know you were trying to defend your territory during the battle, but ... Anyway, we have a difficult task ahead of us, and could really use your help."

Midnight lines up in the row between Greg and Daniel. He walks in step with them on the deserted road.

They pass an abandoned SUV. It has been stripped of tires, side mirrors, and the carpeted floor mats, but they still check for anything of value. They are reduced to scavenging like everybody else. Lin finds a Beatles Sgt. Pepper's music cassette in the glove compartment.

"Leave it. There are no batteries or electricity to play it," Daniel says.

Lin puts it in her pocket anyway. She's always had a soft spot for the Beatles.

As they round the next curve, the lake spreads out in front of them. The encampment on its borders has grown. It now stretches all the way past the dam toward Sunrise Highway and the Laguna Mountains. People are desperate for water. They have cut down most of the old-growth trees that lined the lake to use for firewood. Wood they need to boil the water and cook meals.

"These trees were the only survivors of the great Cedar Fire in 2003," Greg says. "It will take decades for them to grow back."

Daniel nods sadly.

"It looks like a refugee camp," Lin says.

"It is a refugee camp," Daniel answers. "And we are the newest addition."

"No Daniel, we're not refugees, we're here on a mission. We are going to win our home back. We are fighting for our family. The battle was lost, not the war. Got it, Daniel?"

"Okay, Dad."

"We need to find out who's in charge here. Guard your water bottles and the supplies we brought. They're more valuable than gold these days. Follow me."

Lin fingers the switchblade in her parka pocket. She's ready to defend herself if necessary. She has to pick her way carefully around people sitting lethargically in front of their tents, or under strung up tarps. No one looks up. A few children play by the lake, but even they seem lackluster in their pursuit of an empty soup can.

Lin steps over discarded bones, plastic bottles, empty bags, pieces of torn clothing, dirty diapers. The smell of urine and feces is so strong she has to pull her bandana over her nose.

GREG:

Greg stops to get the lay of the land. This camp, like every group of people, has a hierarchy. Someone gives orders, and others obey. There are those who profit, and those who pay. He needs to find the people in charge. And fast. Vega's life hangs in the balance.

It doesn't take long, before a group of three young men carrying rifles walks up to their group.

"You can't come here. We're already bursting at the seams, and we have no resources to share," says a man with greasy hair shot through with gray, and an over-grown scraggly brown beard.

Midnight barks at him and takes a protective position in front of Greg.

"We're not looking for handouts. We're here to help you." Greg is conscious of the fact that he does not have a beard like every other man. He was able to shave only two days ago.

"Where do you come from, promising help?" The bearded man laughs.

"We live here. I'm Greg, and this is my son, Daniel, and his girlfriend, Lin."

"What a lovely family. Y'all look clean and well-fed. What do you want with folks like us?" He turns around to his companions, who laugh at his remark.

"And who are you?" Greg continues unperturbed.

"Pardon me, but we have more important things to worry about than meeting the neighbors."

His two companions, grungy in dirty jeans and plaid shirts, laugh again at their leader's joke.

Greg lips twitch almost imperceptibly. "We'll be on our way then. Find someone who's interested in our proposition." He turns to go, and Daniel and Lin follow.

"Hold on, Greg," the man hollers. "I'm Matt, and this is Bo and Derick. We'll hear you out, but we won't promise not to take your nice clean backpacks and sleeping bags from you. It seems we have the upper hand here."

"You could do that, Matt and Bo and Derick, but I don't think you will. Because it would only give you short-term relief. What I have to offer is a long-term solution."

"You hear that, fellows? A 'long-term solution!' I haven't heard that word in ages. Here we just live from one day to the next, heck, mostly from one hour to the next."

"Precisely. Take me to the person in charge, a place we can talk."

"I can barely stand the tension. I'm pissing myself with curiosity!" Matt mocks, and Bo and Derrick laugh again. But he moves into the camp, and Greg, Daniel, and Lin follow. Along the way, people make cat calls at them. "Nice boots!" someone shouts. "Expensive jacket!" "What's in the fancy backpack?" "Got any food, cigarettes?" "Hey, cutie! Welcome to the camp!" followed by raucous laughter.

Greg notices Lin tightening her grip on Daniel's hand. He regrets bringing her. It won't be easy to protect her.

Before long another group of four men blocks their way.

"Hey Matt, what're you doing with these newcomers? Can't just keep them all to yourself, you need to share."

"Out of my way, scum," Matt answers and tries to swipe the heckler aside. "We got important business to discuss."

"Oh yeah, what kind of 'business'? You're just a puffed-up bully!" The provoking man, who has oily long brown hair, grabs Matt's hoodie and pushes him to the ground. The other guys in his gang holler and attack Matt's buddies Bo and Derrick. Matt fires his rifle into the air.

Everyone freezes. Women grab their children and push them into the tents. After a second, Oily Hair laughs and kicks Matt's rifle out of his hand. One of his buddies grabs it and points it at Matt's head. Oily Hair stomps his foot onto Matt's chest, immobilizing him.

Greg needs to diffuse the situation fast. Should he just quietly make himself scarce with Daniel and Lin and leave the fight to this bunch of knuckleheads? Or should he intervene, help Matt to resolve the situation and get him on their side? It would be nice if Matt and his guys owed him. They have weapons and they are aggressive. But how?

"Gentlemen," he says, which gets him smirks all around. "This is a misunderstanding. I am the reason for this brawl. I am the 'business' our friend Matt here spoke about. I'm willing to cut you into the deal, if you will take me to your leader."

"Take me to your leader," Bo and Derrick intone mockingly.

Oily Hair looks confused. "What deal?" His momentum is broken and his trigger hand is unsteady.

"That's what we're here to discuss. So, why don't you point that rifle at the sky, and let Matt get up?'

"You can't tell me what to do!" Oily hair shouts and waves the rifle back and forth wildly.

Greg grabs the gun barrel and pushes it up. "I would never presume to tell you what to do. I just respectfully ask that you take me to the camp leadership and hear me out."

"Camp leadership? What the fuck? I guess he means, Gordon," Oily Hair mumbles.

"Of course, he means Gordon, you nitwit," Matt says. He scrambles up and tries to restore some of his hurt pride.

Oily Hair hits him in the face, and Matt stumbles but finds his footing again.

"Give me back my gun." They struggle for the rifle and a shot goes wide into the air.

"Dad, these guys are idiots," Daniel whispers into his ear.

"Shh, they're all we have to work with right now. Let's go find this Gordon."

He can't waste his time with these imbeciles while Vega is teetering between life and death back at the dugout. He slowly backs away from the cursing and fighting, and they make their way carefully through the tents.

"Gordon would live in the best tent, probably a large stand-up tent, probably by the lake. Look for a nice tent away from the riffraff and the stench. It should stand out," Greg tells Daniel and Lin.

"I would live on that island in the middle of the lake if I had the choice. Good overview and easy to defend," Lin points to an elevated island with tall pine trees connected to the main campsite by a narrow dam and a bridge. They can see a checkpoint at the entrance to the island, manned by five armed guards.

"Fletcher Island. Good thinking, Lin." Greg feels his stomach contract into a hard rock. How are they going to get onto the island past the guards? And how are they going to get off? Tempers are high and violence runs under a thin surface of civility in this camp.

Daniel echoes his thoughts. "Dad, let's take a break and think this through. We're exhausted and it looks pretty difficult to get onto the island."

"There's another access road over a bridge in the back," Greg says. "Let's make our way along the lakeshore toward the other side of the island. We can rest along the way." Greg doesn't want to rest. He wants to get back to Vega quickly.

"I remember that bridge from our walks as kids," Daniel says. "I'm sure there'll be guards on the bridge as well."

"Let's find out." Greg sets out in a wide curve along the edge of the lake keeping a wary eye on the campers.

The placid surface of the lake sparkles in the sunlight, soothing Greg's frayed nerves. There's still beauty amidst all this ugliness, he thinks just as he steps into dog poop. Greg swears under his breath.

Midnight wags his tail. A few rowboats with fishermen bob on the lake.

"These boats used to be rented out to tourists on the weekends," Daniel explains to Lin. "The lake was stocked with trout. It's been two months since the solar storm. The fish are probably gone by now."

The campers have thinned out on this side of the lake, but Greg still has to step over the occasional makeshift bed or pile of trash. The sun warms his back, and the birds twitter as if the apocalypse had never happened. Greg feels transported back to a time before the solar storm, when Vega and he came up here for the weekends and took hikes along this lake. How is Vega now? His heart clenches, and his eyes lose focus. Is she going to make it? Time is of the essence. He needs to concentrate and get help.

Greg follows a path that leads into a wooded area on the backside of the lake where many of the pines and live oak trees are still standing. Greg can see the bridge is guarded by two patrolmen. The shore of the island on the other side of the bridge was once a popular picnic spot, with a table and a grill. It is now occupied by a family. The smell of grilled meat wafts over to them and Greg feels faint with hunger.

"Let's rest here in the shade and eat."

The underbrush is dense and there's no space for tents. Greg finds a concealed spot with a view of the bridge. They take the food Rose has prepared from their backpacks—sandwiches of black bread and hard salami—and eat hungrily. Greg takes a slice of salami and gives it to Midnight, who's sitting at his feet.

"So, what's the plan?" Daniel asks.

"Let's just watch for a while. Figure out when they change guards. What the family is doing. Who comes across the bridge; gather intelligence."

"Okay, and once we get across?"

"I have a gift for this Gordon. One he won't be able to turn down."

"A gift?"

"Right here in my backpack."

Greg stretches his legs and tries to relax his aching back. But before he can get too comfortable the pale face of Vega appears in his mind.

25

DAY 55: STEVEN

The mountain is still dark and dead quiet. Wet dew from the early morning fog hangs in the trees. Last night, Amy's mother Claire found the clearing with the calendula flowers. He and Amy picked as many as they could carry. Afterwards, he got a few hours of sleep, while Claire made an ointment from the flowers in a pot. Now he is drinking a nourishing witch's brew Claire prepared. It gives him strength, even though he cannot identify the pieces of roots and herbs swimming around in it. Reasonably rested, they head toward the beehive, en route to the dugout.

To stay awake and pass the time during the two-hour hike to Kosmik Mountain and the cabin, Steven asks Claire how she learned so much about healing and plants.

Claire wipes the sweat off the back of her neck with a

stained handkerchief and replaces her hat. "I'm a trained nurse and pharmacist. I worked in a hospital in the city before Amy was born. That's where I met Amy's father. He was a patient with a serious gunshot wound. I was in the ER when he came in."

"How did he get shot?" Steven asks, while putting one foot in front of the other on the uneven trail.

"He was a medicine man and an activist of the Inaja tribe, from the Kumeyaay Nation. They had staged a sit-in on a parcel near Juniper, as a protest for having been robbed of their land. As a medicine man, Amy's father was not allowed to carry a weapon, but the Feds shot him anyway."

"Why?"

"Because he was a leader and he had power."

"Mom, why didn't you ever tell me about my father before?" Amy stops abruptly and faces her mother.

Claire looks at Amy unflinchingly. "I was afraid to tell you," she says quietly.

"Afraid of what?"

"I was afraid you'd run off looking for him and I'd lose you." Claire's stares at the ground in front of her.

Steven feels like an intruder in this mother-daughter moment. He takes a step back to give them some space.

"And now, you're not afraid anymore?" Amy challenges her mother, eyes blazing.

"No, now I think you'll stay." Claire looks at Steven, who blushes. These women are intense.

"Continue the story," Amy starts walking.

Finally. Steven's all into intimate revelations between family members, but they have to get to Vega.

"Leonard was recovering on my floor at the hospital and as soon as he was strong enough to travel, the Feds were going to arrest him and throw him in jail. They planted a guard in front of his room." Claire picks out the trail between shrubs and trees.

"Sounds pretty exciting." Steven is picturing this scenario in his mind as a movie scene.

"It certainly was. I had to distract the guard and then smuggle Amy's father out on a gurney. I took him home to my apartment and took care of his wound until he was strong enough to get up. But I knew it was only a matter of time before they would find him with me. So, I quit my job and we came out here to Juniper, to the little house at the edge of town where Amy grew up. He taught me a lot about native plants and healing methods. When Leonard was strong enough, he went back to his tribe."

"He left you, Mom? After you gave up everything to save him?"

"No, Amy, he gave my life meaning, and he gave me you, the most precious gift of all."

"Does he even know about me?"

"I don't think so. I didn't tell him. His tribe would have never accepted a white woman—and he already had a family."

"He ruined your life—*my father!*" Amy is ducking underneath a low hanging sugar pine branch.

"I don't see it that way. I wasn't happy working as a nurse in the hospital. The patients there were treated like objects in a sterile environment. Leonard gave me a whole new way of looking at the world. He taught me about the power of plants and how to make tinctures. Taught me to look at people as being connected to the earth around them. I was happy living in our little house in Juniper, and many women came to me for help and for healing. We were able to survive—until the Bastards came ..."

"But it wasn't your decision to make, keeping my father from me." Amy stamps her boot in frustration and anger.

"You have his strength and his temper." Claire smiles and puts her arm around her daughter.

Steven listens in wonder. What a wild story, and what a brave decision Claire made. He loves that she led such a renegade life, and is relieved that she has professional nursing skills. But time is passing. "Let's go."

Fifteen minutes later he points across the slope at the wooden box his father built. "Here we are. Over there is the beehive."

He used to watch his parents put on their white bee-suits with the veiled helmets to open up the beehive. They have no bee suits now. Claire winds one of her shawls around her hat and puts on her leather gloves. She asks Amy and him to burn pine needles and dried sage from her bundle in a small clay pot and wave it over the hive. The bees are still quiet this early in the morning, and the smoke makes them even drowsier. With her small knife, Claire pries one of the bars with a full comb teeming with bees out of the box. She brushes the bees off and detaches the comb from the wooden bar, drops it into one of her burlap bags, and replaces the bar to close the gap.

"That should be enough," she says and tells them to extinguish the smoking pine needles and sage. "We're ready for your mother."

Hopefully we're not too late, Steven thinks grimly. "This way," he leads them through the underbrush toward the dugout. No sound from the cabin. The Bastards must be sleeping soundly, and he didn't see anybody on guard duty on the deck when the cabin was briefly in view.

The cracking of branches and their steps on gravel sounds as loud as gunshots to Steven's ears. They have to break through the underbrush. There is only a deer path to follow. It must be close, but it's hard to keep his bearing. Coming out onto a small gap in the trees, Steven straightens his back and looks straight into a gun barrel.

"Jesus, Tarek, don't shoot!"

Tarek lowers his pistol. "Sorry, I had to make sure it wasn't the Bastards."

"You still have ammunition?"

"Three bullets."

"This is Claire, Amy's mother. How is my mom?" He talks in whispers. Sound carries far in the valley.

"Bad, but hanging on."

They crouch to avoid the oak branches until they reach the small clearing in front of the dugout where Tarek kept guard all night long.

Claire looks at the branch-covered entrance. "Is she in there?"

Tarek nods.

"I'm taking Amy inside with me. Everyone else has to stay out."

Tarek pulls aside the branches for Claire and asks Hilde, Eleni, and Rose to come outside. Still groggy from sleep, they mumble greetings to Claire, Amy and Steven before they stumble to the camping chairs and logs arranged around the unlit propane stove.

"And I need hot water," Claire calls from inside.

Tarek lights the propane stove and puts on an aluminum pot with water.

"We'll be out of propane in less than a week," he says to Steven.

Steven just nods. He's exhausted—mentally and physically. He slept a few hours on the hard wooden floor of the shack last night. It was cold and all the bones in his body ache. He would have liked a little comfort and warmth from Amy beside him, but she slept in a corner near her mother.

He feels like a great responsibility is lifted from his shoulder. He has delivered Claire to his mother—hopefully not too late. Now, there's nothing to do but wait.

The air is still cold and damp. He looks at the silent people around him. Eleni sits on her father's lap, both of them covered by a down sleeping bag. Rose sits on a camping chair and puts a teabag into a tin mug. Her eyes are red, her hair is stringy and dirty. Hilde sits erect in another chair. She has combed her short hair, and tries to put on a brave face.

Steven can't deal with these people now. He can't think about the propane running out. He just wants to close his eyes and not be responsible for anybody. He let them down. He knows they wouldn't be in this predicament if his battle plan hadn't failed, but right now he just can't deal with another thing.

Claire calls again for the hot water, and Tarek takes the battered aluminum pot off the stove and passes it to Amy inside the dugout.

"It's good you found Amy's mother. Vega couldn't have hung on any longer," Hilde says.

"She thinks Jack's killer was a woman," Stevie answers. "Claire was with Jack when he died."

Steven looks at the women in the circle around him. Rose has a bad temper, but she wouldn't be able to keep killing a man to herself. If she'd killed Jack, she'd be hysterical. Vega, the great pacifist could never hit a man over the head with a rock. Inge, may she rest in peace, was such a kind and gentle soul, and she wouldn't have had the strength or height for such a violent attack. He looks at Hilde sitting across from him. Hilde looks like she's about to cry but she doesn't. She looks back at him and meets his eyes defiantly.

"The propane has not run out yet," she says. "We still have provisions. It is not winter. The Bastards have not found us yet. We are still alive. As long as the worst has not happened yet, I will not cry."

Steven gives her a tired smile. Rose looks up briefly, her eyes blank. Then she goes back to stirring her tea.

But what about Lin? Lin is fierce. She's a warrior princess. Steven wouldn't put it past her to bludgeon a man if she considered him a threat. Steven remembers her lack of reaction when they found the body. Almost as if she wasn't surprised. She just heaved Jack over the rim without a moment's hesitation.

26

DAY 56: VEGA

Vega is burning up. Her face and body are so hot, she feels like she's in an oven. But when she looks up, green branches stretch overhead. Where is she?

An unfamiliar face appears in her field of vision. It's a woman her own age; she has dark hair streaked with gray. Her kind face smiles at Vega and says soothing words she cannot understand. Claire or Clara. Vega knows these words mean light. Behind the face, rays of light stream through the green branches. Oh good, she found the light again. Vega smiles back. The kind woman puts a cool compress on her forehead. It smells like honey and lemon and some kind of flowers.

"Calendula," the woman says and shows her an orange flower. "Here, sip this." The woman, whose name means light, holds Vega's head up and puts a mug of tea to her lips. "Drink, it's garlic, turmeric and calendula—natural antibiotics."

Vega feels her heart rate going down, she can breathe easier. A pleasant coolness trickles from her forehead through her body.

Beams of light form a halo behind the woman's face. Vega decides she is in the Bardo, the transit station after death, and the woman is the benevolent deity Tara, the goddess of compassion, who resides in this in-between realm.

"I will treat your wound with aloe vera, and an anti-inflammatory propolis paste. You have a slight infection, but I can heal you. Rest peacefully now."

Vega relaxes. Amy is waving a small bundle in front of her. Vega can smell sage. I wonder why Amy is here, she thinks just before she closes her eyes and floats off into space again. Hears voices as if from a far. "Amy ... turmeric paste ... calendula ointment..."

Someone touches her side with gentle fingers. It hurts, but Vega is so relaxed, she barely flinches. Her body is being washed with a sponge and warm water. A sweet, high voice chants a silvery tune. Maybe Tara. The woman applies a compress to her side. A cool, calming essence penetrates her body. Maybe it's okay to return to her body. Maybe her body is not done yet. Maybe she can return to Greg and her sons. Light filters through branches above. It flitters and shimmers.

27

DAY 56: GREG

By 9:30 p.m., the half-moon sends its pale light across the lake and illuminates the bridge. The trees cast an eerie moon shadow, concealing Greg's location. Two guards are leaning on the bannisters of the bridge. One is sitting on the rough wooden planks, smoking. It's the end of their shift. Greg can tell they are tired.

He looks at Daniel and Lin's dirt darkened faces and nods. Their backpacks are packed and ready.

"Okay, Midnight, go!" Daniel sends off the dog.

Greg makes a silent plea for the black lab to do its job of distracting the guards and not follow his own undecipherable agenda. Midnight runs to the bridge, tail wagging. The guards see him coming and get up to face him.

"Let's go!" Greg signals the command and stealthily they creep to the moat under the bridge and begin wading through.

"What are you doing here?" one guard asks Midnight, who starts to bark.

"Where do you belong?" the other guard asks.

Midnight makes an assortment of noises, between barking, howling and whimpering. Non-threatening noises.

"Where are your people? Who do you belong to?" The guard sounds friendly, like he is leaning over the dog and inspecting him for a collar.

Greg, Daniel and Lin have reached the other shore. They are about to climb out of the water and onto the embankment. This is the tricky part. There is no cover.

Cause a distraction, Midnight, Greg silently pleads.

"You want to play, don't you?" one of the guards says and laughs.

Midnight is doing a good job.

Crouch low, run to the cover, Greg signals to his people. They run up the slope to the tree line in the moonlight.

"Hey, who's there? Stop or I'll shoot!" one of the guards shouts.

They keep going.

A shot rings out in the quiet night.

Greg, Daniel and Lin throw themselves into the

bushes. A guard is running in their direction. So is Midnight.

Greg feels a rough arm pulling him out of the brush and a gun barrel is jammed into his temple.

"Who are you? What do you want?"

A dirty, bearded man pulls Greg up to a standing position by his parka collar.

Greg raises his hands, so the guard can see them. "I have a message for Gordon. I am unarmed."

The second guard searches him, while the gun barrel remains firmly on his temple.

"No strangers are allowed on this island. Gordon has more important things to do than to meet with you," the guard who pulled him up snarls.

"I have a gift for him."

Two more armed men come running down the hill, alarmed by the gunshot.

"Good you're here. We have an intruder," says the first guard to the newcomers.

"He says he has a message for Gordon. He's unarmed."

"Okay, let Gordon decide what he wants to do with him. You march him up there. We'll take over the bridge."

Greg silently pleads they won't discover Daniel and Lin.

Midnight comes up to Greg, wagging his tail. He's obviously very proud of himself. Greg reaches down to pet his head.

"That's your dog? You're lucky we didn't shoot him."

With a gun barrel now in his back, they walk up the hill to the center of the island.

A few minutes pass in silence. Greg hears music and laughter coming through the trees. Unfamiliar sounds in a camp like this. Few here have reason to celebrate.

On a clearing, a tall stand-up tent comes into view. It is lit from within. Outside the entrance two more guards are posted, with rifles at the ready.

The tent has been decked out like a general's command post at a medieval battle field. Two standards are fluttering in the night wind. One blue and the other red. Except they are not made of silk or embroidered cotton, these flags have obviously been ripped from a parachute or a canvas cover. The tent itself has been painted with crude graffiti with black and white latex colors. The symbols of an acorn, a bow and arrow, a large sun, wavy water, and a simplistic crown are covering the tent's nylon surface.

Apparently, Gordon considers himself the king of the woods, the lake, and the sky. Greg registers these clues. The symbols look comical, like the work of children, but they may be helpful in negotiating with the camp leader.

"We have a prisoner to bring to Gordon," one of the guards says and pushes Greg forward toward the tent's sentries. "He claims to have a gift for Gordon."

"I'll find out if he wants to see him."

Leaves them waiting outside in the mild night. Where are Daniel and Lin?

"Okay, bring him in."

He's pushed inside the tent, and forced onto his knees.

In front of him sits a large and corpulent man on a makeshift throne, cobbled together from rusted pipes, wooden branches, semi-precious stone, locally found felspar, rose quartz, and leopard rocks held in place by wire. The man, who must be Gordon, has a bloated face with a bulbous nose, glistening from alcohol or sweat, and salt-and-pepper hair in a short militaristic crew cut. Short hair and shaved cheeks are rarities reserved for the privileged. Gordon has both. His small beady eyes glint cruelly at Greg. Greg bows deeply before this pseudo-king of the forest, who actually wears some sort of crown, made from cut and bent aluminum, and a red cape probably made of tent canvas.

The scene is too bizarre to comprehend. In one corner of the tent, a 'bard' is playing the guitar and a girl with long blonde hair, wearing a floor-length floral dress, is singing a ballad by Bob Dylan. A dozen people in quasi-medieval garb stand around in a semicircle and clap to the beat.

Gordon raises his hand, and everybody falls silent.

"Prisoner," he addresses Greg. "What are you doing on my island?"

"Great leader of the sky, the forest and the lake," Greg responds, feeling very foolish. He's still kneeling and bowing. "I come in peace, and I bear gifts."

"I like gifts. Who are you?"

"My name is Greg, and I own land in these mountains."

"Very well, so you want to pledge your allegiance to me?"

"Yes, great leader, I want to pledge my loyalty and ask for your protection," Greg says. "I brought you a gift as a sign of my respect and acknowledgement."

He opens his backpack under the close scrutiny of the sentry and pulls out a bottle of aged, single malt Scotch whiskey.

"May I approach and give you this very special and old beverage, worthy of kings?"

"No need. My servant will hand it to me." Gordon nods to the sentry, who brings him the bottle.

"Indeed, Laphroaig, 27-year limited edition Scotch, one of my favorites. Let's drink!"

He holds up the bottle, and a servant brings plastic glasses on a tray and pours the whiskey. Greg is invited to partake. He toasts Gordon and they empty their cups.

That went pretty well so far, Greg thinks, but now comes the hard part. I've just given him a gift, now I want something from him.

"So, vassal Greg, where is your land?" Gordon asks jovially.

"It is close to here, on the other side of North Peak on Sugar Pine Road."

"Then why are you here, and not on your land?" Gordon asks.

"Because our land is currently occupied by enemies." Greg motions to the servant to pour Gordon another glass of whiskey.

"Oh, that is a problem. There are enemies everywhere nowadays." Gordon turns around to clink glasses with the blonde girl. "Sing us another tune, my songbird!" he coaxes.

How do I get his attention back? Greg thinks desperately.

There is commotion at the tent's entrance, voices, a shuffle.

"What's going on out there?" Gordon calls impatiently.

The two sentries push Daniel and Lin into the tent and roughly force them down onto their knees.

"We just found these two lurking outside," one sentry reports.

"Three intruders in one night? I must double the guards on the bridge, or replace them with more competent men." Gordon's voice has lost its jovial tone and turned angry. Greg flinches.

"Do you know these people?" Gordon addresses Greg.

"Yes, your Grace. This is my son Daniel and his bride, Lin."

Greg sees Daniel and Lin's lips twitching as he introduces Lin as Daniel's bride. Who cares? He has to get through to this Gordon by any means.

"What are you doing here?" Gordon barks at Lin and Daniel.

Lin raises her head. "Your Highness," she says and gets everybody's attention. "I propose a toast to leader Gordon, and in his honor, I would like to perform a sword dance."

The sentries look doubtful. They only carry guns.

"But you have no sword. Does anybody have a sword?" Gordon's cheeks now glow red from the whiskey.

One of the bystanders in a homemade tunic, hands Lin a cheap plastic sword. She takes it with flourish and nods to the musician to play a tune. He strums the guitar and Lin begins the dance she practiced with Stevie during their training. She pulls out the ribbon from her hair, so it flows and streams freely. She turns and jumps and waves the sword through the air in graceful curves. Her feet barely seem to touch the ground. A wide circle opens, and the bystanders begin to clap to the beat of the music. Lin's hair swishes around her head like a wave.

"Bravo," Gordon cries and claps his hands.

Lin bows flamboyantly, and returns the sword.

"Wonderful! A princess of the East!" Gordon shouts.

"Your Grace," Greg manages to say, inwardly cringing. It's excruciatingly difficult for him to ask for help, especially from such a buffoon. "We need your help!" he presses out between tight lips. Now is the moment. Lin set the stage. "We need to defeat our enemies, so we can share with you the treasures and fruits of our land." He ends with a bow, feeling ridiculous, but he has to do whatever it takes.

Gordon laughs. Not the expected and hoped-for reaction.

"We don't wage war. We already have everything we need here. Our kingdom is complete. We rule in peace and prosperity. You can come back and make offerings, but now we want to retire. It has been a long day. You may go."

Gordon yawns, takes off his crown and hands it to one of his servants. He gets up, nods to all the people present and retreats out the back to another tent. Two sentries carrying candles follow him. He leaves Greg standing in the middle of the tent with Lin and Daniel at his side. Two guards move toward them and escort Greg, Daniel, and Lin roughly out to where they came from. Midnight, who has waited outside the tent, falls in step with them. Down the hill they go, across the bridge where they are uncere- moniously dumped back into the forest where they started out a few hours earlier. Greg's backpack is lighter, without his special whiskey, but otherwise they have accomplishing nothing.

"That was too bizarre for words," Daniel says.

"Very," Lin agrees.

Greg looks back at the bridge they have tried so hard to cross. The first gray smudges of dawn appear at the edges of the lake. Another day and night have passed without getting any closer to winning back the cabin and saving Vega.

"This was our one chance to get help, and I blew it," Greg says quietly

"What else could we have done?" Lin asks defiantly.

Daniel puts his arm around her, but stays quiet. Greg knows he's not used to seeing his father hopeless and defeated.

Midnight is rubbing up against Greg's leg. Daniel bends down to scratch him behind the ears. "It's not your fault, Midnight. You did good."

28

DAY 56: STEVEN

Steven dozes in his camp chair after delivering Claire to his mother. He hears subdued chanting from inside the dugout, and the faint scent of burning sage makes its way into his nostrils. His muscles relax and his mind starts to unwind. He's done what he could. Now he must wait and protect the dugout. He has Greg's Glock in his left hand.

Eleni is still sitting on her father's lap. "Where is Midnight?" she asks.

"I don't know, princess," Tarek says.

"What about the chickens? Who's feeding them, Daddy?"

"I really don't know, sweetheart," her father says wearily.

The sun comes out and warms their quiet circle.

Steven stretches his muscles and holds his face up to the warm rays from above. The woods look so much better bathed in sunlight, he thinks.

Amy comes out of the dugout and pushes a dreadlock out of her tired and drawn face. She sits in an empty camp chair, pours water from the large jug into a mug and drinks.

Steven looks at her expectantly.

"Vega is sleeping peacefully," she says to everybody in the circle. Hilde, who is wrapped up in a blanket, looking stoic, perks up.

"Can I …" Steven begins.

"Her fever is down and mother is treating the infection of the wound."

"What about the bullet?" Steven asks.

"The bullet did not rupture any organs. It's safer to leave it inside than trying to extract it under these condi-tions," Amy explains.

"You can't just leave a bullet inside my mother," Steven protests. Even Tarek looks alarmed.

"Why not? There were hundreds if not thousands of Civil War veterans who survived and lived with bullets in their bodies to a ripe old age," Amy declares.

"Really?"

"Yeah, really. It's looking good for Vega. She's most likely going to make it."

Steven's mind dances with joy. Another chance for

Vega, and for him to make things right between them. "Can I see her?"

"Not now. Let her rest. Sleep is the most powerful source of healing. My mother watches over her. She'll make sure her temperature stays stable and her heart rate is not going up too far. She'll let us know when Vega is awake."

Steven feels a wave of gratitude, but wonders where his father and brother are. How can he get a message to them that Vega is pulling through? Are they rounding up enforcements at the camp? Three months ago, he could have just sent them a text message.

GREG

Slugging around the lake in the pre-dawn hours, Greg worries about Vega. Is she getting better or worse?

Daniel doesn't want to spend another hour on the scratchy uncomfortable pine needles by the bridge. They decide to return to the main camp. They still have three granola bars they brought, but they need to purify water with their purification pills. The water bottles are empty.

What a waste. Better not to dwell on it. Just put one foot in front of the other. Just do what's absolutely necessary right now this minute.

"I wonder how Mom is doing," Daniel says.

"I was just thinking the same thing," Greg says.

"Your sword dance was incredible, Lin." Daniel squeezes Lin's hand.

"Not incredible enough."

"This Gordon is a total nutcase," Daniel shakes his head.

"His court seems to like him."

Greg can hear the disappointment in Lin's voice. "We did what we could. Now we just have to move on."

The camp is quiet and they carefully step around tents and sleeping bodies on the ground. It will take a few hours before the sun clears the mountains in the East.

A man with a rifle is slumped over on a chair outside of a circle of tents. Another tired guard. He startles awake as Greg's group passes.

"Who goes there?"

The man challenging Greg to stop looks familiar. Long, oily hair, a grimy Chargers jersey, tight over the bulky belly.

"Did we ...?" The man says, hesitating, and appraising Greg.

"We met before ..." Greg begins, not quite able to place him.

"Of course," the man says, beaming now. "You are the guy with the red Mustang. I'm Tanner, you gave us supplies and your first aid kit saved my daughter's life. She had an infected cut on her arm, and the hydrogen peroxide and triple antibiotic cream healed her wound and her fever."

"Glad to hear it. I'm Greg and this is my son, Daniel, and his girlfriend Lin." Greg points behind him.

"What are you doing here? You had a car, a house, a red Mustang for crying out loud. Why are you slumming it with us folks?"

"We lost our house."

"Sorry to hear that. We don't have much, but we can offer you a meal and a place to rest. Come into our wagon circle."

"Thanks, we can contribute water and granola bars."

"The kids will love that. We ran out of those a long time ago."

Tanner leads them into a circle of tents around a large fire pit, where a woman stokes the flames to boil water.

"This is my wife, Regina, and this is our daughter, Karin."

A girl about Eleni's age sidles up to her mother and looks at Greg with a mixture of curiosity and suspicion.

Tanner bends down to her and points at Greg. "Karin, this man gave us the medicine that made you better when you were sick, after we first arrived here."

Karin smiles at him shyly. "Thank you."

"You're welcome." Greg is quite embarrassed thinking about how little he gave Tanner and his group back then. Considering the entire trunk was full of champagne and cheeses. But at least he made a difference.

"How is she now?" Greg asks Karin's father.

"As well as can be expected under the circumstances. It's not easy to protect a little girl in a camp like this."

"That's what I want to talk to you about," Greg answers. "We can offer you a safe place."

Tanner's wife Regina asks them to sit down on folding chairs and tree stumps around the fire. She hands each of them a cup of tea. "We ran out of coffee a long time ago," she apologizes, "Now we make rose hip or chamomile tea, plants we can find around here."

Three more men come out of their tents around the fire and join them for tea. Greg recognizes two of them from their original encounter. It seems like ages ago, but the solar storm only happened two months ago. Tanner introduces them and then explains to Greg that they have formed a sub-community within the camp for the protection of their families. They share their resources and help each other out.

"We have a couple of weapons to keep the riffraff away. But they are mostly for show. We barely have any ammunition left," Tanner says, and stows his rifle in his tent. One of the other men has taken over guard duty. Daniel and Lin share their granola bars with the kids and women.

"As I was telling Tanner, I can offer you a clean, safe place. Fresh water, electricity, showers." Greg says, looking around the circle.

He has their attention.

"Sounds too good to be true," says one of the men in a brown hoodie. "What's the catch?"

Greg takes a deep breath. Here he goes again, having to ask for help. The last time didn't go well.

Daniel looks at him, waiting for Greg to speak. But Greg is taking his time.

Daniel takes over. "The catch is that we have to reclaim our property from a bunch of Neo-Nazis."

"That's quite a big catch. Where is this property?"

"Only three miles from here on Sugar Pine Road. It's my land, twenty acres and a cabin I built myself." Greg doesn't mind talking about the cabin. "We have solar power and a well."

"There are only seven Neo-Nazis, and they are almost out of ammunition and mostly drunk." Daniel fudged the part about the ammunition. He really has no idea how much ammunition the Bastards actually have.

"Fresh water, electricity and showers, safety for our families," Tanner says. "Hard to believe."

Some of the men nod their heads slowly. They are all in their thirties or forties, and Greg sees their wives and children emerging from their tents cautiously.

"I'm a family man myself," Greg says and introduces Daniel and Lin. "My other grown son, my sister, and my wife are hiding in a dugout on the property with supplies. I'm worried about how long they can hold out."

More sympathetic nods.

"We fought hard," Daniel says, "But we were outnumbered and outgunned."

"We did reduce their numbers significantly." Lin adds with a vicious grin.

Some of the men smile at her.

"Let's have breakfast," Regina says. "Unfortunately, we don't have eggs ..."

"We do have chickens," Daniel says.

"And a vegetable garden," Lin adds.

Greg cringes inside, wondering if any of the chickens have survived and how much of the vegetable garden is left.

"Chickens?" young Karin cries. "That settles it. We have to go."

The men around the circle smile indulgently, weighing their options.

29

DAY 57: STEVEN

I t's early in the morning and no sounds come from the cabin. The Bastards are not early risers. Steven worries about his father, brother—and Lin. They've been gone three days. Are they safe? Are they making any progress? He bounces his leg restlessly up and down, waiting outside the dugout.

Claire pushes aside the branches and comes out of the dugout. She straightens her back and smooths strands of hair out of her face. She has watched over Vega, fed her, hydrated her, and eased her pain for days. Is his mother finally better?

"How is she?" Steven asks with a slight tremor in his voice.

"You can go in and see her now," Claire says and sits down on a chair.

"Thank you for all you did to save my mother." Steven feels a surge of affection for this woman who didn't even know his mother before he dragged her up the mountain. He jumps up and crawls into the dugout and kneels down next to Vega, who's resting on a pad, her head propped up by a pillow. Her face looks rosy and her eyes are clear.

"Mom, I was so worried about you."

"Stevie," she reaches up and touches his cheek gently.

"It's Steven now, Mom. I've grown up these last few days."

"Steven, I like that. I'm so glad to see you. Thanks to Claire, I'm feeling much better. I was in such a fog for a long time. Everything was blurry, and I was floating ..."

"You were pretty out of it. I'm so happy you pulled through." Steven bends over her and takes her hand. "I'm sorry I gave you such a hard time."

"Don't worry. Maybe I deserved it. We both had to grow up. We're both alive, and that's a blessing." A worried look comes over Vega's face. "Where's your dad?"

"He's down at the lake with Daniel and Lin. They're trying to round up enforcements to recapture the cabin."

"But he's unharmed?"

Steven nods. He won't tell Vega, but he can only hope his dad is fine. He hasn't heard from him in three days.

"Everybody else?"

"Inge didn't make it."

"Oh, no! How sad! Poor Inge. What happened?"

"She got shot saving Eleni."

"What a kind and selfless soul!" A cloud has moved over Vega's face as she looks up at the branches above.

"We buried her on the hill."

"She'd love that. She always liked that view and she'll be nearby."

"That's what Dad said."

"But you, Steven, what are you doing here with your old mother? You should be with Greg, helping him."

"I know. I will go now. I wanted to make sure you were better."

"Do that, Steven. I'm proud of you."

Vega's eyes close and Steven realizes she is still very weak. He gets up quietly and goes out of the dugout. As soon as he emerges from the entrance, Tarek puts his fingers on his lips. *Quiet!*

Steven hears it too, noises from the underbrush, subtle, but twigs are crackling and heavy steps advance.

Tarek silently shoos Eleni, Hilde, Rose, and Claire back inside. He stands guard with Greg's gun held ready, Amy at his side. Steven crouches below the trees with the pickax, holding his breath.

A large man breaks through the underbrush into the clearing in front of the dugout. Greg.

Tarek lowers the Glock and Steven comes out of his hiding place. "Dad! Where are you coming from? Where are the others?"

"Quiet," Greg whispers. "I came to fetch you and

Tarek. We need you to reclaim the cabin. And to check on Vega. How is she?"

"Mom is fine. She's coming around. You have reinforcements?"

Greg nods. "Thank God, your mom is okay."

Amy and Claire come out of the dugout.

"Claire healed mom," Steven introduces Claire.

"You have my deepest gratitude, Ms. Claire." Greg bows to the healer. "Can I see her?"

Claire nods. "She's sleeping. Don't wake her."

Greg crouches into the dugout.

"Dad, where are the enforcements?" Steven calls after him.

Greg returns out of the dugout with a big smile of relief. "She's sleeping peacefully. The reinforcements are down on Sugar Pine Road. Get ready. Amy can stay here and defend the women." Greg holds up a Luger handgun.

"I'm going." Amy steps next to Greg. "Mom, can you defend the dugout?"

"Amy, I'm a healer, not a fighter. I made a vow not to take any life."

Amy glares at her mother.

"You go. I'll defend the dugout." Hilde holds out her hand for the pistol.

"You know how to use this?" Greg asks.

"How hard can it be? You keep forgetting that I lived through a world war!" Reluctantly, Greg shows her how to release the safety and pull the trigger He hands her the weapon.

Tarek and Steven fill a backpack with water and food. Eleni hangs on Tarek. "Where are you going, Daddy?"

"We're going to win back the cabin."

"What about Midnight?" Eleni asks.

"Midnight is with us," Greg tells her. "He was very brave and helpful."

"Okay, Daddy, win back the cabin so Midnight can come back and we're all back together."

"I'll do that, sweetheart. You be good and stay with Rose. She'll take care of you." He turns around after a last kiss on top of Eleni's head.

They bushwhack through the forest, behind Greg, but four people moving through the underbrush are not quiet. Steven catches Greg's worried glance in the direction of the cabin. "Don't worry, they won't be up for another two hours," Amy assures them.

They reach the paved road.

Greg points downhill. "They are down there."

"How did you get here?" Steven asks.

"Walked."

"Weapons?"

"A few." Greg marches down the deserted road at a fast clip.

Steven is impressed. He can't believe his is dad managed to round up enforcements, allies, and weapons.

"It wasn't easy." Greg says as if reading his thoughts.

They continue in silence. Steven walks next to Amy. They have barely exchanged a sentence since returning to the dugout with Claire. A tense silence hangs between them.

Finally, Steven says what's really on his mind. "This Jack, so you and him were an item?"

"We were lovers, if that's what you mean," Amy answers defiantly. "You have grown up in a privileged house, with loving prosperous parents. I didn't. I did what I had to do to survive. And I was determined to survive."

"I'm not judging you. I'm just trying to understand."

"You can't understand, Steven. Because until a few days ago, you were a spoiled brat. I learned to accept Jack, and even like him. He protected me, and he came to your mountain to find my mother and reunite me with her. We were planning to run away together and join up with her."

"But then he got killed."

"By someone in your family."

"No, impossible!" Steven raises his voice.

"Quiet, you guys!" Greg warns.

The road curves beneath the shade of mature oak trees. Around the bend are a group of people in a turn-out. Steven sees Lin and his brother sitting on a fallen tree trunk by the road. He runs toward them.

"Stevie!" Daniel wraps him into a bear hug.

"It's Steven now, brother."

"Okay, got it. How's Mom?"

"Much better. Claire saved her."

"Thank God, you found her. I wish I could go and see her now, but we have to finish this first. This is Tanner. You may remember him from when you picked up Hilde's car at the lake."

After the introductions are made, they go over the strategy, which is very simple.

30

DAY 58: GREG

The Lake Crew, as they call themselves, spent the previous day and most of the night resting, getting acquainted and preparing their equipment.

The crew consists of Greg, Steven, Daniel, Tarek, Lin and Amy, plus Tanner's group of seven men. Before dawn, they walk up to the dirt road and approach on foot. In the gray pre-dawn light, they ease around the Bastards' disabled vehicle and Rose's burnt-out car blocking the access road. Carefully they approach the tree with the sensor of the makeshift alarm system. Tarek disables it by cutting the wire. Greg takes a breath of relief.

Silently, they approach the cabin. They only have three handguns, a rifle and very few rounds of ammunition. Instead of brute firepower, they have to rely on stealth and the element of surprise. It is dead quiet. The sky is a rusty gray.

The previous night, they listened to the drunken laughter of the Bastards until long after midnight. It carried all the way down the hill, to their staging area, amplified by the acoustics of the valley. Greg motions the crew to a halt. He quietly points to the sleeping guard outside on the deck. Tanner nods and waves his men forward.

Greg creeps up the steps, his key in hand, but finds the front door unlocked. Silently, he and Steven enter. Greg counts six Bastards sleeping on the ground and the one outside on the deck. They're all here. Steven tiptoes around the snoring bodies to open the patio doors to the deck and the balcony, so the enforcements can stream in from all sides. A team of two Crew members chooses a Bastard each as a target. One Bastard wakes up groggily. A gun is pointed at his head. Before he can get up, his hands are tied behind his back. But he shouts and struggles.

Daniel and Lin are collecting the weapons to store them out of reach on the patio, next to the gagged and bound guard. Daniel drops a semi-automatic. Now all Bastards are wide awake. Tanner and his son try to contain a Bastard with greasy long black hair. He kicks Tanner's son in the face. Tanner's son lunges at the him. Both tumble over a fallen chair onto the floor. Three members of the Lake Crew separate them.

"Hey, what's going on?" Redbeard barks next to Greg.

Greg is ready for him. He holds his Glock to Redbeard's head and clicks the safety switch. Steven tries to tie his hands. Redbeard kicks and screams, but Greg punches him in the chin with righteous anger.

"Hey, man, what are you doing here?" Redbeard slurs. He tries to get to his feet.

"You thought you'd get away with this?" Greg counters and pushes him back down onto the floor.

"Nice place you had here, whatever's left of it." Redbeard spits on the floor

Greg stands above him and lifts his fist to hit him in the face, but Daniel holds him back. "Dad, don't!"

"Why not?"

"Great wine cellar. We finished it," Redbeard mocks.

Anger surges through Greg. He aims his Glock at Redbeard's head again.

"You killed my mother."

"You killed Jack."

"No, we didn't!" Greg feels blood rising in his face. His right hand is shaking. He has to pull the trigger now, or he won't be able to aim.

"You're gonna kill me?" Redbeard taunts. "Go ahead. I don't think you can do it."

"We don't want to kill you. We just want you gone," Daniel says calmly and puts his hand on Greg's arm. Greg shakes him off, but lowers his gun.

Amy comes running with a roll of duct tape and tapes it over Redbeard's mouth. "Shut up your big, fat shit-face!"

She kicks him in the stomach with her combat boots. He groans. "I never want to see your ugly face again," she yells.

Greg shakes himself out of his rage. "Out, all of you," he yells. "Daniel and Tarek, go downstairs and make sure nobody's left there."

"You're gonna let them go?" Amy challenges him. "How can you? You know what they did to us?"

"Amy, let's talk about his later," Steven says.

"Help tie them up!" Greg shouts.

The Bastards on the ground are kicking and screaming. Their hands are now tied behind their backs. But one gets up and rams his head into Tanner's stomach. Tanner moans and staggers backward. Two of his men pull the Bastard back and knock him out with a few well-placed chin hooks. He falls to the floor. Amy runs like a fury between them, yelling for them to shut up. She puts duct tape over their mouths.

Greg hears noise from the basement. A shuffle, shouts, a gunshot.

"Steven, go downstairs and see what's going on."

Steven leaves.

On the deck all the weapons are piled up. Tanner has recovered and stands next to the assault rifles. He picks one up and fires a shot into the air.

"Out, or we'll shoot anyone left here." Tanner puts his boot onto the pile of the Bastards' weapons. "Three, two, one ..."

"Go to hell where you belong!" Amy yells at them.

"We're keeping all the weapons!" Tanner screams. Amy grabs a semi-automatic rifle. Steven runs over to her and puts his arm around her. "Amy, it's okay, they're leaving."

"How can you just let them go?" She aims her rifle at Redbeard.

"... and zero!"

"We have all their weapons and their vehicle, and we have a lot of people on our side. They are no threat to us anymore."

"No!" Amy screams. "They will always be a threat!"

The Bastards are on their feet, hands tied, and the Lake Crew pushes their gun barrels into the back of the stragglers. They herd them up the driveway.

"If you ever show up here again, you're dead!" Amy shouts after them.

Redbeard turns around and shoots her a vicious look. But he can't scream, and he can't spit. The duct tape holds. Blood drips from his forehead.

STEVEN:

The double doors to the basement are open, and Steven hears grunts, and heavy breathing. His brother's high-pitched voice, "Let go of me!"

What is going on? Are Daniel and Tarek fighting with each other? Since their falling-out over Lin, and

Tarek running away, they haven't been talking. Steven rounds the corner until he sees the chaotic scene inside. A Bastard they had not accounted for is at Daniel's throat. Tarek is trying to pull him off. Steven aims his gun.

"Let him go, or I shoot!" he calls out, but the three men don't hear him. They are too entangled for a clear shot and he can't hurt Daniel or Tarek.

Tarek pulls at the Bastards shirt, cutting into his neck. The Bastard rams his elbow into Tarek's stomach. Tarek groans. Daniel's choking. He's lying underneath the Bastard and now Tarek has collapsed onto the two of them.

Steven fires his gun at the wall.

The Bastard flinches. Tarek uses the break to aim a kick at the Bastard who loosens his hold on Daniel.

"Let go of me, you freaking Arab," the Bastard hisses.

"Don't mess with me," Tarek shouts.

Steven approaches and hits the Bastard over the head with his gun. He collapses and rolls off Daniel. Tarek gets up, breathing heavily. Daniel coughs and pulls himself up to a sitting position.

Steven rushes in to tie the Bastard's hands behind his back with duct tape. He helps Daniel up. "You're okay, brother?"

Daniel nods. "Thanks to Tarek.'

They look at the unconscious body on the ground.

Tarek shakes his head. "That was close."

"You saved me," Daniel is getting up from the floor and looks at Tarek.

Tarek and Daniel stand unsteadily, facing each other.

Daniel extends his hand. "I'm sorry about what I said to you. You belong here."

"It was Steven who knocked him out." Tarek looks at the hand, and looks at Daniel. He takes his hand. "Your family saved Eleni and me."

Steven herds the bound Bastard up to join his comrades. He wants to give his brother and Tarek a moment.

The last thing he sees is Daniel and Tarek shaking hands vigorously. He can't be sure, but it looks like Daniel leans in for an embrace.

31

DAY 58: TWO HOURS LATER: GREG

They chased the Bastards up the hill to Sugar Pine Road toward Juniper. After two hours it was all over. And only two shots were fired into the air—including the shuffle downstairs. They obviously miscounted the number of Bastards.

Now, the men and two women assembled in the cabin breathe heavily. The adrenaline is still running high.

"We did it!" Steven shouts. "We kicked them out!"

A collective cheer rises up from the crew.

"Thanks to you," Greg points to Tanner and his men. "I wish we could toast with a bottle of champagne, but I fear the Bastards have polished off all the alcohol. From now on, this place is yours as well."

Steven interrupts, "Actually, there are still a couple of bottles of single-malt whiskey in the dugout."

"Good, we'll celebrate tonight then. Go to the lake and get your tents and families. Take the Mustang. You can set up below the cabin on the grass under the trees."

"The Bastards will be back," Amy mutters. "You should have finished them off."

Tanner nods. "We'll leave a couple of extra men here until we're back. Just in case. We have plenty of weapons now."

Greg shakes Tanner's hand, and the two men slap each other on the back. "It's a good spot," Tanner says.

As Tanner's men leave, Greg looks around and for the first time he sees the damage. Barely a piece of furniture is intact. But the old, heavy pine table still stands. Broken bottles, spilled liquids and food, torn blankets and pillows, cans, and glass, litter the floor. But the windows are in one piece. The stove and the refrigerator seem functional.

"I'm going to the dugout to get Vega," he says.

"Greg, we need you here, at least until Tanner comes back," Tarek urges him.

"Greg, there seems to be a leak here in the toilet. The floor is flooding," Tanner's son calls for the bathroom.

"I'll be right there," Greg looks downhill toward the dugout longingly.

"Dad, mom is fine. Let's just fix the toilet before she comes. Tarek can go to the dugout and help the women to pack up." Daniel puts his hand on his father's arm.

He shakes him off. "Why did you hold me back when I had Redbeard right in front of me?"

"They let us go, remember. They could have killed us all, when they took the cabin from us."

"Redbeard's still a threat."

"I don't think so. We have enough men now."

VEGA:

Vega wakes up and sees the face of the woman she mistook for the goddess Tara above her, framed by green branches. She now knows the woman's name is Claire. She's Amy's mother, and she is a healer. Vega knows she has saved her life.

Claire smiles at her. "How are you feeling today?"

"My mind is clear for the first time, and my body is barely aching, thanks to you. I'm very grateful."

"Be grateful to Steven and Amy too. They came to find me."

Vega reaches for Claire's hand, and the pain doesn't shoot into her side and back. She can breathe easily and deeply. She hears voices around her.

Hilde kneels next to Vega and hands her a cup of tea. "We're going to move you back to the cabin. The Bastards are gone."

"They're gone?"

Hilde nods. "Greg and Daniel found allies down at the

lake and they helped to win back the cabin. You're going home."

"Where are my boys?"

"At the cabin, cleaning up."

"Thank God. And Greg?" she asks anxiously.

"On his way."

Vega leans back, relieved. Around her, Rose is packing up supplies and sleeping bags. Eleni is collecting her blanket and clothes.

"Come on, Vega, let's get out of this dugout into the fresh air." Hilde and Claire help Vega sit up and crawl out of the low entrance. Vega crouches on the ground in the deep green clearing, taking a moment to catch her breath. The sun on her face feels good.

"Can you stand?" Claire asks. "It would be better for your wound if you could walk up to the house, instead of being carried in a blanket. We'll help you."

"I'll try." Vega gets up and takes a few tentative steps, walking between Claire and Amy, who support her.

The procession winds its way up the hill. First Vega, flanked on both sides. Eleni and Tarek walk behind Vega and her helpers. He's carrying a large bag of rice and a five-gallon water bottle. Rose and Hilde follow, both of them loaded with bags full of cans and dry food.

Vega winces with every step. Halfway up, her legs collapse. They just stop carrying her weight. Amy and Claire try to keep her upright, but she sinks to the ground.

"Get help from Greg or Steven!" Amy tells Tarek.

Claire and Amy drag Vega to the flat rocks underneath her favorite oak tree. It is decked out in his full green leaf-cover, providing ample shade. "I just need to catch my breath." Vega does, and the air feels delicious. She'd assumed she'd never sit here again. It feels like a precious gift and she cherishes the moment with her tree and her rock.

"Take your time, Vega. You'll make it," Claire tells her as she wipes the sweat from Vega's forehead.

Tarek and Eleni run ahead, and from a distance Vega hears barking, and Eleni's delighted response. "Midnight!"

Steven, Daniel, and Greg come rushing down from the cabin.

"Mom, you're up!" Steven sits next to her and hugs her, causing Vega to wince.

"Careful," Claire cautions. "She's still a bit sore."

Greg kneels in front of Vega, and takes her hands. He has tears in his eyes.

"I'm so relieved you're back," Greg whispers. "I wanted to come to you as soon as we kicked out the Bastards, but …"

"It's okay, I understand. You're here now." She leans forward until their foreheads touch.

Steven takes a step back to give them some space. For a moment, they just stay in this position. Speckled sunlight paints shifting patterns through the oak leaves on the flat rocks. A blue jay chirps on a branch above them, as if to say, we're back to normal, back to peaceful.

Vega looks up at Steven. "We each went on our own hero's journey. I went to the space between life and death; Steven, you went to find Claire, and Greg and Daniel went to the lake to find allies. And we all made it back alive and well."

"We had a lot of help. Claire, Tanner and his men, Amy, Lin, everybody came through." Greg says, as he kisses his wife's head.

"Where did you go, Mom?" Daniel asks. "When you were unconscious?"

"I was in a peaceful place. There was light, and I saw my life all at once—when your dad and I were young, after we just met, driving down Broadway in New York, the lights of the city streaming past on both sides like stars in the night. I saw you, Daniel, when you were little with your favorite red hat, Steven with the butterflies on his head in the garden. It wasn't scary at all, it was a wonderful space, but I'm glad to be back."

Greg stands and gently wraps his arm around her waist to hoist her up. "Come on, we'll get you home."

At the cabin Greg settles Vega on the sofa in the view nook propped up on pillows. Rose spread a blanket over it to cover the spots from spilled liquids. Vega watches the clean-up proceed around her, but she doesn't notice all the damage inflicted by the Bastards. Their house is still intact, including the scroll painting of the blue goddess Tara, smiling serenely on her lotus throne, surrounded by pink and golden lotus flowers. Her right hand is extended outward toward the viewer, the gesture of wish fulfilling, helping all those who appeal to her. *Thank you for helping us,* Vega prays silently. The brocade framed Thangka is hanging on the wall, completely unharmed.

STEVEN:

Steven stands on the deck looking down at the tents scattered across the slope below the cabin. He watches Tanner and his men clear a space for a big campfire. Greg gave Tanner his big tent, and they are joking about decking it out like Gordon's tent on Fletcher Island, with standards and flags and a family crest. Tanner and his family can stand upright in the tent, and they have even moved in a table with three chairs, and three mats with sleeping bags around the sides. Everybody is laughing and preparing for the celebration that night.

Amy, and Claire are washing clothes and blankets in a large metal tub. Eleni has already befriended Tanner's daughter Karin, who is her age. They are both playing with Midnight. Daniel is taking down the metal barrier from the deck. Two men carry wood from the lower part of the property to the fire pit. A few others are erecting their tents, bringing in sleeping bags and blankets for their families. Tanner's wife arranges the camp chairs around the fire.

This scene of bustling activity makes Steven happy. It's

almost like being back on a movie set, with so many different people in motion, each doing their job.

Two months ago, that's where he was. It seems like an eternity ago.

He goes inside the house where Vega is resting on the sofa with a smile on her face. Rose is sweeping up food scraps and broken China. Lin scrubs off sticky liquids from spilled drinks with a wet mop. One chair is broken. Feathers from ripped pillows are plastered to the tacky floor. Claire and Amy hang rugs and blankets over the deck banister to air out. It's Tarek's turn in the shower. Hilde washes the dishes. Greg and Daniel are in the basement checking for supplies that can be salvaged. The wine cellar is empty. Steven is collecting trash to take outside and bury.

"How can I help?' Hilde asks, putting a way the last intact coffee mug.

"Make some tea, Hilde. We need it." Rose says in a clipped tone.

Hilde heats water on the stove. She brews a cup of tea and brings it to Claire "You must be exhausted from doing the heavy wash," she says as she hands the mug to the healer.

Steven notices Claire's look of surprise.

"I can't cook, but I can make tea," Hilde laughs.

Claire takes the mug. Smells it. Checks the color, and takes one small sip. Her face transforms. She gags and spits the tea on the floor. "What is this?" Claire croaks. She looks up, horrified. Her expression shows a dawning realization. She points at Hilde. "You did it. You killed Jack!"

Everybody in the cabin abandons their task and turns to watch.

Claire holds up the mug for all to see. "This tea is poisoned. I think dried daffodils bulbs."

"Hilde, what do you have to say?" Steven asks gently.

"I didn't mean it ..." Hilde is shrinking back from Claire.

Claire stands up straight and tall and pronounces loud and clear, "Hilde knows I was there when Jack died. She knew he talked to me, but she didn't know how much he told me. That's why she tried to get rid of me."

Steven looks at Hilde. Vega's mouth is open in complete disbelief.

Hilde's face crumbles and she starts to cry.

"Hilde, is this true?" Vega asks.

"I did it to protect you," Hilde sobs. "You took me in. You gave me a safe place to stay. I didn't want to lose this home again. I did it for all of us. After the war, when the Russians came, my mother had to hit one of the soldiers over the head with a heavy frying pan when he came through our door. She saved us. He would have raped us, taken our food. When I saw Jack's swastika, I panicked. I picked up a leopard rock. He was kneeling on the ground, looking at some flowers. I don't know how I had the strength, but I hit him over the head with the rock. I couldn't stop, I hit him again and again. To save us, to protect us." She breaks down crying. Sinks to the floor.

Steven can't believe his frail godmother killed a man in cold blood. He called her before the solar storm. He brought her out to the cabin.

"Aunt Hilde, you brought the wrath of the Bastards down on us," Daniel says quietly.

"How could you try to poison my mother after she did so much to save Vega?" Amy confronts Hilde with the tea mug.

"Inge told me that the daffodils leaves and bulbs are toxic, that's why the deer don't eat them." Hilde says. "Cleaning up, I found some bulbs in the pantry…"

"Hilde, why didn't you tell us this before?" Vega asks.

"I was going to, but then nobody mentioned the body, so I thought maybe the body was taken away. And then when the Bastards wanted him back, it was too late." Hilde cries.

"But why try to poison Claire? She is a healer; she saved Vega?" Steven is sitting on the floor with Hilde, but he can't wrap his head around what she did.

"I heard you talking at the dugout, Steven, that Claire was there when Jack died. She heard what he said. I thought, what if she knows, what if he told her, and she gives me away …"

"I didn't know anything until now," Claire interrupts her. "All Jack said, was that it sounded like a woman's voice."

"I'm sorry. I'm so sorry ..." Hilde is sobbing again.

"Hilde, you have to leave." Greg says without anger, only sadness. "It's not just that you killed a Neo-Nazi—and I believe that you tried to protect us—but you didn't tell us, and you just tried to poison Claire. There are no authorities to bring you to justice, but you can't stay here with us anymore."

Everybody is silent. Looking at Hilde, a bundle of misery on the floor.

Steven can't help but feel sorry for her. What she did was inexcusable, and she set in motion events that caused so much pain—the battle, Tarek's kidnapping, Inge's death, his mother's injury. He kneels on the floor next to Hilde and puts his arm around her. "I know you tried to protect us, but you caused a lot of damage."

"I told you she'd bring nothing but trouble when you took her in," Rose says defiantly.

"Where am I supposed to go?" Hilde cries. "Don't send me away!"

Steven looks at his father and brother. "Let her stay at the dugout," he says. Vega nods.

Greg's face is without expression, but he doesn't say no.

"Don't send me away," Hilde pleads.

"It's better than going to jail," Rose says coldly.

Steven sits back down next to Hilde. "We'll visit you. We'll bring you food."

"Will you ever forgive me?" Hilde asks.

"You have destroyed our trust in you. I will always love you, and I will forgive you. But not now." Steven hangs his head.

Hilde collects herself and gets up.

"I don't forgive you," Amy says. "You killed a good man, and you tried to poison my mother."

"I can't forgive you either. Because of you, I was a captive of the Bastards and they mutilated me." Tarek holds up his left hand with the missing finger.

"I will never forgive you. You brought all this misery on us. You killed my mother, Inge!" Rose's voice sounds shrill.

"Okay, let's not get overly dramatic," Greg intervenes. "She didn't kill Inge."

Hilde stands shivering in front of her accusers. "I'm sorry," she sobs. "I tried to help."

"Your help usually turns into a disaster," Rose mocks.

"Rose, please, that's enough," Vega interrupts. "You're strong, Hilde. You'll be okay."

Daniel helps Hilde pack up her bag and escorts her to the door and down to the dugout.

A glum silence settles over the cabin after Hilde is gone. Should he go and see her off, Steven wonders.

"So, the mystery is solved," Greg says.

"It doesn't feel satisfying at all." Steven still sits on the floor. He's known Hilde all his life. She's given him money for his birthdays and for good report cards. He can't reconcile the fact that she murdered a man in cold blood for no other reason than a tattoo of a swastika. Maybe it was some long-covered trauma from the war. But trying to poison Claire? He puts his head in his hands.

From the corner of his eyes, he sees Amy sit down next to him. She puts her arm around him and rubs his back. He tries to smile at her, but it doesn't quite come out right.

STEVEN CAN HEAR the victory celebration getting under way down below the cabin. Someone is playing a fiddle and there's a harmonica as well. But Steven is not in a festive mood. Nobody in his family is. He should be ecstatic but Hilde's banishment and departure have put a damper on everybody's relief to be back home. Hilde was part of the family. Daniel left her at the dugout, and made sure she had enough supplies to last a while. He told Steven that when he turned to return to the cabin, she held onto him, pleading with him to stay. It almost broke his heart. He promised to visit, and said Steven would come as well, even Vega, once she was stronger. After everyone had calmed down, Hilde might rejoin them at the cabin eventually.

Steven hears his mom talking quietly to Claire. Vega won't participate in the celebration. She will rest in her newly washed bed in the bedroom. He joins them. Claire is kneeling on the floor next to Vega, taking her pulse and feeling her forehead.

"Pulse is normal, she has no fever. But she still needs rest."

Vega holds Claire's hand and squeezes it gratefully.

"I'm going to sleep in one of the tents for now," Claire tells them.

Vega and Steven start to protest

"I don't like sleeping in a house. Too confining. It's getting warm and now I can make a fire if needed. I'll be close by so you can come and get me any time. When Vega no longer needs me, I'd appreciate it if you and Daniel help me fix up the Goldrush shack. I'd like to live there."

"Of course, if that's what you want, we'll be happy to help you. Will you join the celebration tonight?" Steven asks.

"I wouldn't miss it!" Claire gets up and pushes a strand of hair behind her ear.

Steven carries a huge pot of cooked beans and Daniel brings the rice to the party. The Bastards did not bother to cook rice and beans. Too much work, Steven figures. He's grateful for their laziness. On the lower patio, Greg grills canned sausages from the dugout.

The orange glow of the bonfire illuminates the familiar faces of Steven's family and the still unfamiliar ones of Tanner's group. He sees relief and even some joy in these new faces. They've been through a lot, but they're part of his community now. Steven pours the last of the whiskey into plastic cups. Lin and Amy hand out bowls of food.

Rose stands arm in arm with Tarek. Steven watches her laugh at something he says and shake her long hair back from her face. Daniel sits in a camp chair next to Tanner's son, talking and sipping whiskey. Eleni and Karin perch on a log, petting the one remaining chicken. The girls giggle and stroke Midnight at their feet, head on his front paws, eyes at half-mast.

Greg piles the last sausage on a platter and raises his plastic cup in a toast. "Here's to victory over the Bastards!"

"Victory!" Steven shouts and everybody joins in. He takes a big gulp. The whiskey runs down his throat warm and comforting. He looks for Lin. She is standing next to Amy. They are talking quietly. Daniel walks over to the girls and takes Lin's hand. Steven joins them.

"I want to thank all the people who made today's victory possible," Greg announces. "Tanner and his men and their families. Daniel, Lin, Steven, Rose, Tarek. Here's to all of you!"

Steven takes another sip. It burns in his throat.

"To Amy who fought like a tiger, and her mother Claire, who saved my wife, Vega!" More cheers.

"We'll survive together. We'll work together. We'll hunt, grow food, and we'll protect each other until services are restored and power becomes available again. And once this crisis is over, you'll always be welcome to visit, camp or stay at the cabin whenever you like."

"Hear, hear," the group of people around the fire responds.

Tanner gets up to give a little speech. "To new friends and to new allies!" He lifts his glass. "When we first met, just a few days after the solar storm, down by the lake, next to a red Mustang, I thought Greg and his son, Steven, were just a bunch of arrogant and entitled landowners who had everything we lacked."

Boos from the Tanner camp erupt.

"But then, Steven here, stepped in to prevent a fight, and I recognized a deep decency in father and son. Granted, they could have helped us more, back then ..."

Shouts of "yeah," and "yes, please" from the Tanner camp, and Greg cringes in embarrassment.

"... but ..." Tanner holds up his hand to quiet the crowd. "... they did help us some, and they saved my daughter, Karin, and for that I'll always be grateful."

Cheers again. Karin smiles and blushes on her log next to Eleni.

"Now we have safe shelter, clean water, electricity, and friends. We'll make it through the rest of this disaster together!" He lifts his glass and everybody joins in.

Lin is blasting *Sargent Pepper Lonely Hearts Club Band* from a cassette player. A guitarist starts to play the tune "With a little help from my friends." People sing along. A few get up and dance.

Lin and Daniel swing their hands along with the music.

Amy sings loudly and very out-of-key. "And I do appreciate you being rou-how-ound." Next to her, Steven grins at her Beatles interpretation.

"We have to find a place for you to sleep, Amy," Daniel says to prevent Amy from belting out another line.

"Don't worry, Daniel. Tanner gave me a nice red two-person tent he doesn't need anymore because he's moved into the *big* tent. I set it up with a view and privacy." She turns to Steven. "Are you coming, Steven?"

Steven blushes deeply as Amy takes his hand and leads him away. He lets her.

EPILOGUE

Above the cabin, on the path leading to Kosmik Peak, not far from the spot where Jack had laid, a man watches the celebration below. He hears the music and the laughter, he smells the grilled sausages. He looks through a pair of binoculars, which enable him to see the exact layout of the camp, the number of people present, including children and women. The man smiles and strokes his red beard.

ACKNOWLEDGMENTS

This book was inspired by a cabin we built in the Cuyamaca Mountains. It was completed just in time to ride out the Covid pandemic. While the cities became ghost towns and people were shut down in their houses and apartments, we were able to sit on our spacious deck and breathe clean mountain air. Our ranch became a refuge and sanctuary. Our friends came to visit for an escape from the confinements and restrictions of the cities. But I didn't want to write about the pandemic. We all all are sick and tired of Covid. So, my son Sebastian came up with he idea of a giant Solar Storm hitting the earth and creating massive black-outs and an Aurora Borealis of epic proportions. He also supplied me with the scientific details of the CME, and checked my descriptions of the aftereffects. It became the perfect apocalyptic event for this survival story. If I I got any CME related facts wrong, it's all my mistake.

My son Max gave me valuable developmental editing tips about the battle scenes and the arc of the story lines.

Thank you as always to my writing group members

Kim Keeline, Nicole Larson, Suzanne Shephard, Valerie Hanson, and Tamara Merrill for their feedback helping me to make this story better.

Thanks go to my husband Glen, who inspires me with his caring and his competence to build a mountain retreat from scratch

ABOUT THE AUTHOR

Cornelia Feye is an art historian, author, and publisher. In 2016 she and her husband bought land in the mountains and built an off-grid, solar-powered cabin. It is the inspiration to the story *Refuge on the Mountain*. Fortunately, the worst disaster they had to weather at the cabin so far was the covid pandemic.

If you enjoyed this survival story, please consider leaving a review on Goodreads or amazon. Or check out our website for brilliant novels by Cornelia and other Konstellation Press authors.

www.konstellationpress.com

Printed in the USA
CPSIA information can be obtained
at www.ICGtesting.com
JSHW022312141223
53781JS00004B/80